Justine,

A Date with

By: Kira Adams

Copyright © 2015 Krista Pakseresht. All rights reserved.
http://kristakakes.blogspot.com
https://www.facebook.com/KiraAdamsAuthor

Cover designed by Cover Me Designs
Editing by Joanne LaRe Thompson

This book is a work of fiction. Names, characters, places, and events are the product of the author's imagination or used in a fictitious manner. Any resemblance to actual persons or events is purely coincidental. No part of this book may be reproduced or used in any manner without the written permission of the publisher, except by a reviewer who may quote brief passages for review purposes only.

Don't forget if you're not doing something you love, you're not really living!

♡ Kira Adams

This is for all the women and men out there
in the world that can relate. Never let anyone
treat you with less respect than you deserve.
You control your destiny.

One: A Point of No Return

I knew deep down inside there was a possibility he would take it to that dark place, I just never admitted it aloud. I knew if I did, it would become real and I had been living in my own lie for so long; I didn't want to believe it.

It isn't until I smell the gasoline that I know we are at a point of no return.

"What are you doing?" I sputter out, gasping for breath. My ribs ache, and I have a splitting headache. I am blinking rapidly in an attempt to gain my bearings. I can feel the cold, hard concrete beneath me and I realize I am lying on the ground outside. The wind stings my face, sending goose bumps throughout my entire body.

Why can't I move?

Fear begins to accelerate through my bones at a rapid rate. I can feel my heart beating ferociously against my chest.

Why can't I move?

I'm still blinking continuously, hoping this is all just a bad dream.

"You should have listened, Bryce. You never listen."

I rack my brain quickly trying to remember what, if anything I did wrong this time. That's when Tyson's face pops into my head. Tyson was going to be my accomplice tonight. He didn't know it, but he was going to help me escape this hell I've been confined in for the past couple of years.

I swallow loudly.

He warned you, my inner voice scolds me. The same voice that has held me frozen in fear in our relationship for the past two years.

I'm looking up at Robbie, and I don't even recognize him. His eyes are cold and dark, his expression blank.

That's when I see the match. He flicks it across the back of the holder and a flame ignites.

"No! No! Please!" I'm squirming around, but excruciating pain is shooting throughout my entire body.

"Just remember Bryce, you did this to yourself."

And then he drops the match.

* * *

A year later...

"Bryce!" I hear my mother call up to me. "Dinner's ready."

I instantly drop the book I've been engrossed in for the past few hours, slip a sweatshirt over my head, and make my way downstairs.

I follow my nose to the dining room to find the table already set and my parents standing together in the kitchen in front of the stove.

"Come on, dish up," my mother tells me, her brown eyes on me as I walk toward the plates and retrieve the four which are set at the table.

"Mikey!" my mother yells, attempting to get my brother's attention.

"Coming!" my younger brother's voice carries from upstairs.

Stroganoff is a family favorite, and my rumbling stomach tells me I'm going to enjoy this meal more than I normally would.

After dishing up my food, I make my way to the dining room table and take a seat just as I see my brother walk in.

He's bouncing happily toward the plate my father holds out to him. "Good of you to join us."

Mikey shrugs, his long curls obstructing his view.

"Did you finish your homework?" my mother asks as she hands him his plate back, now piled on with food.

He nods then joins me at the table. After my parents are seated, we go around the table sharing the events of our day. It's my least favorite part of dinner.

"Bryce?" My father looks up from his plate expectantly at me.

I push around the food on my plate with my fork. "I looked for jobs today."

My mother's chocolate eyes widen as she keeps them trained on me. "And?"

"And nothing…I was just looking." It's the same conversation we have been having for the past two months. Somehow, my mother never seems to lose hope that they can be rid of me soon. They already raised me once; it isn't the most ideal situation with me being *back* at home.

They've been beyond understanding and supportive. They knew I needed a safe place to heal and adjust, but they never expected me to stay as long as I have. They haven't come outright and said it yet, but I feel it.

The fact that I haven't left the house since I moved back home over ten months ago is also a deterrent for them, I'm sure. My parents already had their hands full with Mikey—they weren't anticipating me.

Mikey was an honest mistake. They had me when they were in their early twenties and were convinced I was going to be an only child. Not for lack of trying. Mikey was their miracle child, conceived fourteen years after me.

After I flew the coop at eighteen, I never imagined returning home for anything other than the normal holiday stays. You can say it's been a difficult transition. Living with your parents at age twenty four? Not something I care to brag about…

It's hard to live with people I don't have much in common with. The age difference between Mikey and me plays a big role in why we aren't closer. He's at the stage where all girls have cooties. There are times when I wish we connected more. My parents both work full-time jobs and are gone ten hours or more a day.

"How's Tyson enjoying ASU?" my father asks.

"He likes it. He joined an intramural softball team."

"Oh cool." My mother's eyes light up.

"What's intramural?" Mikey asks, his dark brown eyes questioning.

"It means girls and boys play for fun," my father answers.

"Will Tyson be stopping by tonight?" my mother asks. She has told me multiple times how good she thinks it is for me to be around people, namely Tyson. I'm sure she hopes he'll eventually rub off on me. I wouldn't hold my breath.

"No, he's got a game tonight."

"Maybe we could all go cheer him on?" she offers up, but I can tell she is treading lightly.

I nod slightly. "I'll tell him you guys want to stop by."

My mother's expression falls. "Bryce, you can't hide forever…"

I've suddenly lost my appetite. "May I be excused?"

My brother has been unusually quiet during the entire dinner but suddenly, he seems to have found his voice. "May I be excused too?"

I can hear my mother sigh, dejected.

I don't wait for permission, just clean off my plate and make my way back to my room.

The first thing I do is check my cell phone for text messages. Sure enough, I have one waiting for me from Tyson. *How's your day?*

I reply with *Meh*. It's the same answer I've been using for months.

It's a beautiful day, you sure you can't make it to the game?

Even though he knows my answer already, he attempts to get me out of the house at least once a day. I really can't fault him for it. What sane person stays indoors for twenty-four hours a day, seven days a week?

Only people named Bryce Turner…

In my defense, I went through a very traumatic event and I am dealing with it as best I can. My therapist says I'm making progress, so that's all that counts. My mother had to search high and low for a therapist who would make home visits. Luckily, she eventually found one in Linda Xavier.

I've been seeing Linda for nearly six months, and I feel fortunate that I really like her. Believe me, I've heard horror stories about therapists, but Linda is far from scary. In fact, her demeanor is so warm and inviting, I instantly felt like I could trust her. She comes every Wednesday at four.

I wish she came more often because she really is the only human interaction I get besides Tyson and my family.

She never pressures me to talk about my past. Some days we just sit in silence, but I always leave feeling better because I am with someone. We've spoken about Robbie and that day, but she knows to tread lightly because it is such a sensitive topic for me. It doesn't help knowing that he is out there somewhere…probably waiting to finish the job. If it wasn't for Tyson, I wouldn't be here today. He saved my life…although, some days I wish he hadn't. I can't tell you how many anxiety attacks I've had during her sessions, but she never faults me for it. She never makes me feel guilty. That's why I really like her.

I stand in front of my mirror, lifting up my sweatshirt to expose my damaged body. I ended up with third degree burns on forty percent of my body. The scars that remain are leathery and discolored. Besides my family, no one has seen the extent to which I've been injured…and I'd like to keep it that way. I would hate to see the pity in their eyes, if anyone else got a look.

Two years ago, I loved my body. Yes, I had flaws like anyone else, but I could wear a bikini any day of the week and pull it off. My cellulite wasn't highly noticeable and I liked my small frame. My mother used to tell me that she gave birth to me, so she was to thank for my cute figure.

I can't imagine wearing a bikini or shorts ever again. My legs, arms, torso, and back are littered with scars. I have no idea how my face made it out unscathed, but I thank God everyday he spared it. It's the only thing I have going for me these days.

I've been through more surgeries than I can count, but I will never be able to get back to the girl I used to be. She died when that match was lit.

Tyson, my one and only friend, was my next door neighbor at the time. He moved in next door to Robbie and me before it happened. We had only conversed a few times, but Robbie had convinced himself that there was more going on. Besides borrowing the usual eggs and flour, we kept our distance—until the day he heard my screams. By the time he made it outside, Robbie had fled the scene. Tyson had a hell of a time trying to put out the fire before the paramedics showed up.

We've been practically inseparable ever since. It's funny how you can live your life next door to someone and never know that you need them until that fateful moment. I don't know what I would have done without him throughout this past year. He's one of the only bright things in my dark life. Although he is two years younger than me, I never notice the age difference. He's honestly my favorite person in the world.

Before

* * *

"Are we really going to do this tonight?" I ask, closing the door and locking it behind me. Robbie won't even look at me. He hasn't said a word since we left his friend's barbecue.

He continues ignoring me, walking further into the house. I hate when he shuts me out like this. It drives me nuts. *"Hey! I'm talking to you!" I call out to his back.*

Robbie spins around, his eyes narrowed and his jaw tight. If he opens his mouth, I fear he'll bite my head off with one quick movement.

He's so outta line, and he doesn't even know. He has convinced himself that his friend Jason was flirting with me back at the barbecue and he is pissed. He's been pushing me to admit it since he saw Jason touch me on the shoulder. I never felt uncomfortable, and Jason always treats me respectfully, so Robbie is not getting the outcome he so desperately wants.

"Look, babe, I forgive you," I say proudly, reaching out for him.

Robbie pulls away, a disgusted look playing across his face. "You forgive me?" he asks angrily. "I didn't do anything wrong."

The world will literally have to end for Robbie to admit his mistake. He is as stubborn as they come. I've learned over the past year to simply agree with him and drop it. You have to take the good with the bad, right?

"You're right. So, I'm sorry, let's move past this." I say gently, pulling him into me. He smells like the cologne I bought him, Kenneth Cole, Reaction. It's one of my most favorite smells in the entire world.

He pushes me away from him roughly. "I don't want you wearing this kind of stuff anymore." He points to my basic tank top and jean shorts. My eyes glance down at my outfit and back at him. I can't help the chuckle that escapes my lips. Robbie's eyes darken. He doesn't say a word, just locks his jaw.

I have no clue what's wrong with the outfit I have on, but if Robbie thinks he is going to tell me what I can and can't wear, he is going to have a rude awakening. I push his hand away. "I am going to wear whatever the hell I want," I say, emphasizing my freedom.

Before I even know what is going on, Robbie has backed me up against the cold, hard wall. He is in my face and he doesn't look happy. His fingers are wrapped around my throat and I'm so shocked, I'm having trouble moving. "You're a grown woman now, time to start acting like it," he hisses at me through clenched teeth.

I am trembling beneath his tight grasp. My heart is pounding in my ears, drowning out all other noises. I close my eyes, breathing deeply, attempting to gain control of my fleeting heart.

I begin coughing, gasping for air. I feel his fingers slowly release. "You know how I get," Robbie says, a distressed look plastered across his face. "But you still push my buttons."

I'm rubbing the soreness his fingers left around my neck. I can't believe he put his hands on me. I can't stop shaking. I push past him without another word, headed upstairs. He grabs my wrist stopping me.

"I'm sorry. I'm sorry. Please forgive me." He is groveling, on his knees, pressing the base of his head against the back of my hand.

His shoulders are heaving up and down, and I can tell his breathing is uneven. I can feel your fingers around my neck…and you're the one that's crying? *I'm flabbergasted. I want to scream, yell, punch, and cry. A thousand emotions are rising from the depths inside me.*

I'm not supposed to be this person…a girl who is too weak and allows someone to put their hands on her. I'm better than this. I deserve more than this.

"Baby, please, please, just look at me," Robbie begs, *gripping both my hands in his, tears streaming down his face.*

And somehow, I still feel sorry for you...like I wronged you somehow. *I pull my hands away, digging my nails into my palms. I feel dirty for even considering forgiving him. I feel disappointed.*

He reaches up his hand to my face, and I flinch from the caress. He chokes on a sob, turning his head away from me, his eyes tightly closed.

I can't believe you put your hands on me. *The warm liquid is pooling beneath my eyes, trailing down my face. Robbie reaches out for me one more time, and I lose it.* "Don't touch me!" *I scream, and then race out of the room and up the stairs to our bedroom.*

I can hear the barreling footsteps behind me. I should have known I wasn't getting away that easy. "Bryce! Bryce!" *Robbie cries out frantically. He's desperate to fix his mistake. Everything is just happening so fast. I need a moment to process what just took place.*

I race through our room, hurriedly to the bathroom and slam the door behind me, locking it. Seconds later, I hear the frenzied knocking by Robbie. "Bryce, come on, let me in! I'm sorry. I didn't mean it."

My heart is still beating wildly as I throw myself onto the sink, gasping for air. I think I'm having a panic attack. Between tears, coughing spells, attempting to catch my breath, and regulating my heart beat, I'm a mess. I don't understand how, in a matter of a couple of minutes, everything I thought I knew about my relationship with my boyfriend was turned on its head.

Robbie is a hothead; something I learned very early on within our relationship, but we've been together for fourteen months now, and besides the occasional screaming in my face and blocking my movement, he's never taken it further physically...until today. Things have been escalating recently. I know he's been under stress from his job, and he's been going through some recent family drama, but it doesn't excuse the fact that he tried to choke me.

Last week, during a heated argument, he called me a worthless piece of shit and spit in my face. He apologized profusely and promised he would never do it again...but it killed me inside. He thought low enough of me in that moment to spit on me like I was trash. I've never felt lower in my entire life. I almost left him. In fact, I had even started packing, but Robbie is a master manipulator. Not more than a few hours later, we were on the couch laughing and kissing, like nothing had ever changed. He doesn't know I cried myself to sleep that night. I felt like such a coward for forgiving him.

All I could think of was how much time we had invested in each other already. Starting over seemed...complicated. Robbie pounds harder, startling me. "Bryce!" he's becoming more agitated. I'm not sure what he will do if I don't open up. I glance up at the door which is reverberating from the rough pounding.

I press my forehead against the door, my heart in my throat.

How the hell did we end up here?

Two: Overcoming Hesitation

"So, you missed an epic party this weekend." Tyson's dark eyes light up.

We are seated on my bed, eating popcorn and watching an action flick he picked up from Redbox on his way over.

"Is that so?" I ask, popping a few kernels in my mouth. "Tell me all about it."

"Well...you remember how I told you about my buddy Jeff and his girlfriend Andrea?"

I nod. He's mentioned their relationship troubles a couple of times. Let's just say it doesn't sound like the healthiest thing they have going.

"Well, everything kind of came to a head at the party when Jeff found Andrea in bed with another guy!" Tyson's voice is gaining momentum, and he is smiling, making his eyes twinkle. I love how animated he gets when he is telling a story. I live vicariously through him and his adventures out in the real world.

"Shut up!" I basically spit out the popcorn from my mouth. "So, then what happened?"

"He beat the shit out of the guy and dumped her in front of everyone at the party."

"No way." I am shaking my head. I wish I could have been there to witness it. Hearing him tell me about it almost makes me feel alive.

He is nodding, chuckling. "You would have paid to see that break-up!"

We both bust up laughing, causing my sides to hurt. "I bet you're happy that you don't have to listen to him bitch and moan anymore."

"You have no idea." He sighs, lacing his fingers behind his head and leaning back. "So, what's new with you? Any good books lately?"

I know the last thing he wants is to hear about the romance books I let myself get lost in, but I still appreciate the fact that he asks.

"Linda gave me a new assignment."

He seems to perk up at my statement. "Oh, really? What is it?"

"She wants me go check the mail every day. She said that by next week when I see her, she wants to see my progress." I swallow deeply, attempting to keep my heart rate in check. Just the idea of stepping outside sends my anxiety through the roof.

"That's great, Bryce." Tyson pauses, sensing that I'm uncomfortable. I swear it's a sixth sense of his. He's always careful not to overstep his boundaries. "Have you attempted it yet?"

I shake my head "no" slowly.

"Well, if you don't take the first step, you'll never start. Want to do a practice run today?" I'm surprised Tyson puts up with me. I'm surprised he even likes spending his time cooped up inside with me. If I were in his position, I'd be out and about enjoying the world around me. Not that I'm complaining or anything.

My heart rate is accelerating, and I'm stressed that he can hear it from his position beside me. I wouldn't be surprised if he can see my heart beating out of my chest. It's pounding so loud in my ears, I bet I'm going to end up with a migraine.

"I don't think I can do it." I move the popcorn bowl away from me, and look down onto my bedspread.

"You didn't even try," Tyson says softly. I can

feel his eyes burning into me…willing me to look up.

I swallow again, attempting to buy more time.

"Come on, I'll go with you. You don't even have to take a step outside if you don't want to. Let's just try to make it to the front door…deal?" His voice is so calm and soothing it's difficult not to want to do it, even just for him.

Slowly I nod.

"Is that a yes?" His voice seems to have jumped a few octaves.

I giggle nervously, finally allowing myself to lock eyes with him. He is grinning widely.

He doesn't waste any more time, jumping off my bed and grabbing my hand. "If we wait, you'll just change your mind. Come on."

He's right. *How does he know me so well?*

I let him pull me off my bed and we make our way downstairs.

Just as we hit the area rug that sits in the entryway, my inner voice begins to scream at me.

You can't do this. Turn around and go back upstairs.

I double back, attempting to quickly race back up to my room before he notices, but I am not quite fast enough. His hand has a tight grip on my arm, and I am not able to escape. "I'm right here with you, Bryce. We haven't even opened the door yet. You can do this."

I find comfort in his soft tone. I squeeze my eyes tightly, as I hear him begin to turn the door handle. I let his words wash over me, drowning out the sound of my beating heart. *You can do this, Bryce.*

I can feel the sun on my face for the first time in over a year, but I keep my eyes closed. I'm afraid of what will come next.

"Open your eyes," he whispers softly into my ear. "I won't let anything happen to you, I promise."

Slowly, I open one eye at a time and my neighborhood comes into focus. There is a little girl riding her tricycle down the street. Birds are chirping loudly and there isn't a cloud in the sky. Seems like the perfect day. I breathe in deeply, wanting to commit this to memory.

"How are you feeling?" he asks, rubbing my shoulders.

"Normal." And for the first time in a long time, I believe it.

Before

* * *

"Where were you?" Robbie demands the moment I step inside the house. His grey-blue eyes are cold as ice.

"I stayed at my parents'," I reply, shoving past him.

"Really?" he asks angrily. "Because I called your parents' house and they said they hadn't heard from you this week."

My stomach plummets. You called my parents' house? *I feel like I'm reporting to my father, not my boyfriend. I don't bother replying as I head toward the stairs.*

"Let me see your phone!" Robbie holds out his hand, his eyes wild.

"What? No," I reply instinctively. I'm not a child. I refuse to be treated like one.

I needed time away from you. Don't you get it? You're suffocating me. I'm slowly dying inside, and you're the cancer.

Of course I've tried leaving Robbie multiple times, but he's threatened suicide, he's followed me around like a sad puppy-dog for days, and he always promises to

25

change, but never does. Our relationship is so unhealthy, I don't even remember what normal feels like.

Honestly, I worry that no one will want me now that he's broken me down into nothing. I feel worthless, unworthy. I can't remember the last time I felt beautiful or loved, happy or content. If Robbie knew that I stayed with my friend Scarlett last night, he'd be convinced that we hung out with guys behind his back. He already hates Scarlett, and thinks she's a bad influence on me. I wish I would have put more stock into what my friends and family thought of Robbie before staying with him for over a year and a half, it's really saying something when no one likes him. I always gave him the benefit of the doubt—acted as if they were judging him unfairly, but now I am beginning to see things they've told me since the beginning. Robbie tries to isolate me and brainwash me, and it's been going on far too long. I need to leave him, but it's the most terrifying thing in the entire world.

"You slut," Robbie hisses at me, his eyes fixated on my phone. I can see a vein in the side of his neck, bulging out. His jaw is tight and locked, and he is grinding his teeth back and forth.

Ding Dong.

His head swivels around, his eyes cast in the direction of our front door. I'm literally saved by the bell. He stalks over to the door and swings it open. A guy with shaggy dark brown hair and chocolate brown eyes stares back at him. He's got a few inches on Robbie. The guy is dressed casually in a patterned tank top and jean shorts. To say he's handsome would be an understatement. His eyes flip back between Robbie and me. I take a few steps toward the door, curiosity leading the way.

"Hi there!" The stranger waves with a bright smile.

His smile is absolutely contagious, I find myself returning it with an equally warm grin.

"I'm Tyson, I just moved in next door. I just wanted to take a moment to say hello and let you know that if you ever need anything I'm just a hop, skip, and a jump away."

I giggle internally at how adorable he is. His eyes linger on mine and I feel a volt of electricity shoot up my spine. I swallow, my heartbeat increasing steadily.

"Thanks," Robbie says shortly and then begins to close the door. Tyson throws his arm out, intercepting it.

"I also wanted to give you guys the heads up that we are going to have some people over tonight, and it may get loud. If it gets too loud for you, can you please let us know?" What a proactive neighbor.

Robbie grunts in understanding and then begins to close the door again.

"If you two aren't doing anything, you should drop by, have a cold one," Tyson manages to call through the crack in the door before Robbie shuts it in his face.

Robbie turns back around to me.

"That was rude," I point out. "He wasn't even done talking and you were already closing the door in his face."

Robbie's eyes narrow. "We're in the middle of a serious conversation. I don't give a crap about some fucking party."

I sigh. So much for saved by the bell…

Three: Paralyzed by Fear

The idea of my assignment is so much easier to digest than the actual action of walking outside for the first time in over a year. My house, my room: they've become my safe haven. A place I know I am protected from the terrors of the outside world, protected from *him*.

"So, how is your assignment coming along?" Linda asks, seated across from me in our study. She tucks her honey-colored curls behind her ear.

It's Wednesday, unfortunately for me. It seems to have snuck up on me faster than I'd imagined it would. Normally I look forward to seeing Linda. Not this week. This week I've been dreading it like the plague.

When Tyson took me for the test run, I felt like I could do anything…but after he left, I attempted my assignment at least three more times with no such luck. By the time my right foot crossed the threshold, I began to hyperventilate. It was the same, each and every time. I gave up after that. It's too hard, and I can't do it.

I shrug, avoiding eye contact. My eyes land on

the picture frame behind Linda's head. It's a family portrait that was taken only a couple of years ago, but I don't recognize that girl in the photo. Her smile is genuine and real. The portrait is obviously from a happier time.

"Bryce, did you even try?" It hurts hearing Linda doubt me. She hasn't judged me since she first stepped foot into our house, and I really look up to her.

My eyes shift back to her. "Yeah," I say in a small voice. "I tried...I just, can't do it."

"What makes you say that?" She is holding her notepad away from her, too focused on me to write. Her brown eyes fixated on me.

"I tried it...okay? I'm just not strong enough," I snap back at her, guilt instantly washing over me as I realize she is not to blame for my shortcomings. "I'm sorry."

"You have nothing to apologize for." She always lets me off easy. Sometimes, I wonder if she were stricter with me, would I be making more progress than I have been? But I can't imagine having anyone else as a therapist, so I try to push those thoughts to the back of my mind.

"Tell me what ran through your mind when

you attempted it. What made you think you couldn't do it?" Of course, even with my outburst, she keeps pressing on.

"That he is going to find me."

"That is a valid fear. What makes you think he's still out there?" I've answered this question over a hundred times, but she still continues to ask it. I'm positive when she does, she is hoping for a breakthrough. Unfortunately, I never deliver.

"Because they never found him; he vanished without a trace."

"Do you believe he's still in the state?" Another valid question I've been asked previously.

I shrug. "I don't know."

"So, it's the fear of the unknown? Do you miss being able to leave your house?"

"What kind of question is that? Of course I miss being able to leave my house like a normal person. To not have to feel like I constantly have to look behind me every second of every day...but this is my life now, and I've accepted it." Although these questions are not new to me, today, they irritate me more than usual, grinding on my last nerve. It could be because

I just started my period, it always puts me in a foul mood…but it could also be because this is the closest I've been in a year to stepping outside, and I just don't have the strength to go through with it.

She handles my resentment with grace, keeping herself composed. "I think that's enough for today. But Bryce, I want you to remember that you don't have to settle. Your life is what you make of it. You're only a prisoner if you let yourself be."

I'm not sure she is supposed to say these things to me, being a therapist, but we have a deeper relationship and I appreciate that she doesn't always color within the lines.

I nod and watch as she begins to pack up her notepad and pen into her purse. "Same time next week?"

It's never changed since we began our sessions, but I like that she double checks. Not that I've ever cancelled on her, I yearn for the interaction too much for that.

"Yeah, see you then."

I stay seated as I watch her walk out the double doors and into the entry way. I hear the front door open and then close behind her, followed by silence. My parents won't be home for another hour, and Mikey has soccer practice after school, so I am alone with my thoughts.

I'd give anything to be able to get in my car and just drive somewhere. My car has been sitting inside the garage since I moved home. I slowly make my way to the garage door, opening it slightly, then turn on the light inside. The light shines down upon my Honda Civic LX. It's an older model, four door, and teal. Although it doesn't have all the bells and whistles of the newer versions like automatic locks and electric windows, I love it all the same. I always have. In the eight years I have owned it, it has only broken down two times. I nearly totaled it once, but my insurance was able to reconstruct it, and I never noticed much of a difference.

I step out onto the cold floor of the garage and run my hand over the top of the roof, closing my eyes. I don't even remember what it's like to drive with my windows down, the wind whipping through my hair. Opening the front door slowly, I slide in, feeling the familiarity as I sit behind the wheel. I slide my fingers over the steering wheel, gripping it and releasing, letting myself get lost in memories.

I hear a loud bang and my heart jumps into my throat. I'm out of the car faster than I can blink, barricading myself inside the house and locking every door. I don't know what the noise was or where it came from, but I am not going to be investigating it. It sounded like a loud pop, possibly a gunshot or something else equally loud. It has my heart beating wildly. I race upstairs to my bedroom, closing and locking the door behind me. Climbing into my bed, I pull my comforter up to my chin. It always seems to soothe me. I'm still shaking, but my breathing is beginning to return to normal, my heartbeat slowing.

I grab my phone off my nightstand and notice a missed call from Tyson. He's probably dying to hear how my assignment went. I haven't been completely honest with him. When he asked about it earlier in the week, I told him I was making progress…but now I feel guilty for lying to him.

Before I can rethink it, I am dialing the familiar number. He picks up on the third ring. "So, how did it go?" The enthusiasm in his tone is more than apparent.

"About that…"

"Bryce?" he asks, in a stern tone.

"I couldn't do it."

"What do you mean you couldn't do it? I thought you said you were making progress?" he presses.

"Yeah, I kind of lied." I'm biting my lip anxiously, nervously awaiting his disappointment.

"Kind of lied? What does that even mean?"

"Okay. Fine. I lied. Happy now?" He has made me completely forget how terrified I was a moment ago and now I am up and pacing across my room.

"No. You lied to me. Why didn't you just tell me the truth?" His tone sounds hurt, I don't blame him.

"Because I was afraid you would be disappointed in me."

"Bryce." He sounds sad, defeated even. "I could never be disappointed with you."

"Really?"

"Yeah, really. I mean, it would have made me happy...really happy if you had completed the assignment. But, I think no less of you." *It would have made me incredibly happy too...believe me.*

"What are you doing?" I ask, desperate to change the subject.

"Homework." He sighs. "I have a huge test on Friday."

"I should probably let you go, then. I don't want to distract you." I've stopped pacing and am now seated on my bed.

"I can take a few minutes out of my day to talk to you. Plus, I need a distraction. I feel like I'm going cross-eyed." He chuckles, bringing a smile to my face. I'm happy he doesn't want to hang up right away. Talking to him has been the best part of my day so far.

"Your parents still planning on taking that trip to the beach?" he asks. They've been wanting to get away for a while now, but they've been too worried about leaving me by myself that they've forfeited any chance they've had to be alone. I can tell they need it though, so when they came to me with the idea, I urged them to go. I don't want to hold everyone else back. I want to stop being viewed as a burden.

Mikey coincidentally has a weekend soccer retreat, so it's going to be me and my lonesome. I'm not exactly looking forward to it. The idea of being alone and vulnerable scares the living shit out of me. Granted, nothing has happened in over a year, but still.

"Want me to come stay with you?" Tyson asks.
God, yes.

"You don't have to do that." My tone is not very convincing, but I don't want him to feel like he has to babysit me.

"I'll be there Friday by four. Leave the door unlocked."

I smile to myself. *This is why you're my best friend.*

Before

* * *

My heart is beating so ferociously, it feels like someone is taking a jackhammer to my chest. My eyes are shifting nervously around the room, darting to the clock and back to the task at hand. Robbie is going to be home any minute. If I don't leave now, he won't let me leave.

I scoop up the bag I just spent the past half an hour packing, glance around at the rest of the belongings I am leaving behind, and say a silent goodbye. This has been my home for the past two years. I'm going to miss it. Just as my foot hits the top stair, I hear the loud roar of his engine. I know without a shadow of a doubt, I'm too late.

I begin panicking, my legs not working properly. If he finds me here, I don't know what he'll do. I swallow, my mind going to the bruises he's left on me recently. Enough is enough. *I race down the stairs as quickly as my feet will carry me, headed straight for the front door. As soon as I swing the door open, my face is assaulted with harsh winds. I carry my bag close to my chest and refuse to look back as I hurriedly make my way to my car. I hear Robbie's door to his Ford pickup close and I feel the adrenaline kicking in.*

"Bryce!" he calls out to me, and I know I've been

caught. I pick up my pace, focused on one task, getting the hell out of here. I don't even have the doors unlocked when I feel his firm grasp on my arm. "Where are you going?" he asks, his eyes wide and frightened. They are shifting between me and the bag, nervously.

I swallow. "My parents are going out of town and they asked me to house sit. It should only be a couple of days," I lie, desperate to escape the hell I've been living in.

Robbie squints his eyes as if he is dissecting the lie I just told him. "I just ran into your mom today and she never mentioned anything like that to me."

"What do you mean?" I ask, surprised.

"I ran into her at the grocery store early this morning and she invited us to dinner this weekend." I doubt the honesty in his words. My parents can't stand Robbie. My mother is the one who gave me the courage to leave. She doesn't know he's been putting his hands on me, but she does know how unhappy I am. She told me I've lost my excitement for life—and she's right. The fact that he is trying to make me believe she was friendly with him is suspicious. Cordial would make more sense.

Robbie grabs the bag from my hands. "Are you leaving me?" he asks, something flashing across his eyes.

I wouldn't be surprised if he can hear the frantic beating of my heart. "No," *I say slowly, the shakiness in my voice evident.*

"Oh. My. God," he accentuates each word separately. "You're leaving me."

I swallow. "I just need some time...to think," I lie. There is only one thought running through my mind: get out.

Robbie's vein pops out in his neck and his eyes go dark. Next thing I know, a fist is coming straight at me. I duck fast enough that his hand meets the driver's side window and it shatters, pieces of glass strewn about the inside of my Honda. I'm shaking, my eyes shifting to my broken window and the blood stained on it.

"You can't leave me!" Robbie cries hysterically, his hand cut up and bleeding. "We are soul mates!"

I want nothing more than to hop in my car and drive away, but he's slowed me down. He's never going to let me leave.

All common sense goes out the window, and my body takes over. Forget the bag. Forget the car. Don't let him win. *I take off in a run down our street, my Converse slapping against the pavement. I can hear his heavy footsteps behind me, but I don't dare turn around. "Help!" I cry out, running down the middle of the street.*

A tear streams down my cheek as I feel his arms wrap around me tightly and he pulls me down to the ground with him, crashing roughly against the hard pavement. Pain shoots through my shoulder instantly and I cry out in agony. Robbie clasps his hand over my mouth, stifling my cries. "You're going to get up, and you're going to walk back to the car calmly. You're going to pick up your bag and you're going to come back into the house with me, understood?"

I'm trembling underneath him. You were so close…

I'm scared what he's going to do to me behind closed doors. I'm scared to face his wrath. I know he is going to make me pay.

Four: An Innocent Game of Truth and Dare

"You sure you are going to be okay here alone?" my mother asks, a worried look spreading across her face.

"I'm sure. Tyson is coming over soon, he's going to stay the weekend with me." She seems satisfied with my answer, but her face still shows concern.

"Alright, call us if you need anything." She hands my father her suitcase to load up in the car and hugs me tightly.

"Mom, I'll be fine. Enjoy yourselves. You deserve it."

She releases me, giving me a tight smile. "See you in two days."

They are gone soon after. I walk around the quiet house, peeking quickly in every room. It's something I've been doing since the incident. It makes me feel more secure knowing I've checked all possible areas. Our house hasn't changed much over the past decade, besides some newer furniture, everything has remained constant. I walk into Mikey's room and it looks as though a tornado blew through it. There are dirty clothes strewn about the floor, his bed is unmade, and I can barely see the floor beneath all the clutter. *Some things never change.* I smile to myself, shaking my head lightly. Once finished upstairs, I head back down to the main level and check the windows, pulling the blinds shut.

Tyson will be over in less than an hour, and although I'm antsy being alone, it's not terrible. I make my way to our study where a mahogany grand piano sits. It's been forever since I've played. I used to take lessons when I was a little girl but after I refused to practice, my parents cancelled them. It was understandable. There is only one song I still remember from start to finish, Beethoven's Fur Elise. My fingers instantly fall on the ivory keys and I let the music take me back…back to when things were simple in my life and back when I had a zest for life and a need for adventure. It feels like eternities ago.

I don't even hear the front door open or Tyson sneak inside behind me. I'm too lost in my own world. When I finish, I feel eyes on me. I turn around slowly, realizing that for the first time in what feels like forever, I was able to forget about my troubles and worries, and forget that I am not normal and will never be again. Remember a simpler time.

"You never told me you could play," Tyson says softly, setting his duffle bag on the floor and approaching me.

"It never came up." I shrug, closing the piano lid and standing up from the bench.

"Don't stop on account of me." He holds up his hands in surrender.

"I'm not." I look down at my feet sheepishly. "That's just the only song I know."

"Well, you could have fooled me." Tyson smiles a toothy smile back at me. "So, what kind of trouble can we get into while your parents are away?"

I'm not much of a rebel and honestly, never have been. Considering we can't even leave the house, our options seem very limited.

I look around the study, pretending to be deep in thought.

"That's what I thought!" Tyson exclaims. "Good thing I came prepared." He walks over to his duffel bag, unzips it, and begins shuffling around inside.

"What are you doing?" I ask, coming up behind him, attempting to get a better view.

Swiftly, he pulls out a bottle of vodka. "Ah-ha!"

I can't help but grin. He really wasn't kidding. "But it's only us...how much fun can it really be?"

"It will only be lame if we allow it to be." He jumps up and begins heading to my kitchen.

I follow as he opens the cupboard and pulls out two small glasses. "Should we do shots or mixed drinks?"

I can't remember the last time I drank, but vodka used to be my drink of choice back in the day, so I shrug. "You decide."

"Shots it is!" He grins widely. He pours what looks to be doubles for each of us and then hands me one of the glasses. "So, we need to make this interesting."

"And just what are you proposing?"

"An old school game of truth or dare." He arches his eyebrows, while raising his glass.

"What are we—in middle school?" I joke.

"Nope, but we are working with what we can. Now, are you in?" He is staring me down with his dark chocolate eyes, and I can't help but giggle.

"All right. But, what are the rules?"

"You pick truth, and I will ask you a question. If you refuse to answer, you have to drink. Same goes with dare, if you refuse the dare—you drink. Sound easy enough for you?" I nod. I have a feeling I am going to be hammered in no time.

"Great! Wanna go first?"

My mind races beginning to think of all the questions or dares I can torture Tyson with. "Sure."

I take my shot glass and make my way to the dining room table. Tyson follows closely behind with not only his glass, but also the bottle, taking a seat beside me.

"What will it be Mr. Richey, truth or dare?"

He seems to debate this for a moment before saying, "truth."

"Do you actually enjoy spending time locked up indoors with me?" I feel bad asking the question, but it's been nagging me for a while now.

He nods slowly. "Yes and no. I like spending time with you, but sometimes I wish we weren't confined to inside these walls."

I feel guilty. He could be hanging out with anyone in the world…yet he chooses to hang out inside with me. "Your turn," I say quickly, wanting to change the subject.

"Truth or dare?" he asks, shifting his glass around on the table.

Surely, he won't ask anything too personal or dare me to do anything too ludicrous…right? "Truth," I answer hesitantly.

"Even though you're my elder, do you find me attractive?" He is flashing me one of his charming smiles.

I avoided those thoughts about Tyson for a very long time. When I finally realized the truth, I was lit on fire. There is no doubt in my mind he can get any girl he wants. Apart from his perfectly styled hair, deep brown eyes, and charming smile, his bone structure is impressive.

I find myself blushing thinking of my best friend in such a way, reaching for the shot glass sooner than I like. I take the shot like a champ, but grimace at the bitter aftertaste.

"Interesting," he mumbles to himself as he sits back in his chair. "Your turn."

"Alright, truth or dare?"

He ponders this for a moment before replying. "Truth." I'm surprised he's taking the safe route.

"What was your first impression of me when you met me over a year ago?" I've been curious for the longest time, especially because Robbie had always been so jealous and overprotective. I always thought Tyson was harmless.

He doesn't even stop to think about his answer, just looks me dead in the eyes. "I thought you were my hot next door neighbor."

The minute the word hot leaves his lips, I'm blushing. I can feel the heat behind my cheeks. *So he thought I was hot.* "Wait a minute!" I exclaim, a realization bubbling to the surface. "Is that why you were always 'out of eggs'?" I use air quotes to get my point across.

"Nuh-uh." He shakes his finger in front of my face. "Only one question a turn. You're cheating. Do you know what that means?"

I shake my head no.

"You have to drink!"

"What? Since when? You never established that as a rule!" I protest.

"Too late—drink up." He pushes my glass closer to me.

I groan. "Okay, fine, but I think you're trying to get me drunk." The alcohol is flowing through my body a few minutes later.

"Truth or dare, Bryce?"

He has already refilled my glass and although I've only taken two shots, I can feel the alcohol warming my body; coursing through my veins. "Dare."

He raises his left eyebrow, surprised at my answer. He begins rubbing his palms together. "Now it's getting good."

My stomach dips as I begin to think maybe I made a mistake.

"I dare you to take that shot in front of you and then another one immediately after."

"You *are* trying to get me drunk!" I point my finger directly in his face.

He chuckles, breaking out into a grin. "*Maybe.*"

I smile at Tyson then down the shot, keeping my poker face tighter this time. He pours me the next one, and it doesn't go down as smoothly. I have to close my eyes tightly and ignore my immediate want to spit it back out.

Now I'm really feeling the alcohol. My head is beginning to feel heavy and fuzzy, and I am giggling for no apparent reason.

"What's so funny?" Tyson asks, attempting to fight off a smile.

I don't even know why I have the giggles, but the more I continue to laugh, the harder it is for Tyson not to join in. Soon we are both chuckling heartily, grabbing our sides from the pain.

"I don't even know what we are laughing at, but I have a feeling I am going to need more alcohol for this." He takes his shot voluntarily before pouring another one for our game. "Whose turn is it even?"

All the laughing has thrown us off track. "I'm pretty sure it's yours, and *I'm* the drunk one!"

"So my plan is working." He laughs an evil laugh and I glare at him.

"Hey! No fair!" I push him lightly in the shoulder. "I dare you to sing 'I'm a little teapot' and dance around this room here!"

His mouth falls open. "I don't even get a choice in this matter, do I?" I shake my head no furiously.

I feel so silly, goofy, and for the first time in a long time, carefree. I can't stop smiling.

He stands up quickly from the table then looks back at the bottle. "Nope, fuck that." Before he decides to take his shot instead.

"Yes!" I say in victory. "My plan is working."

He looks shocked. "This is war!"

I can't help but giggle.

He looks up at the clock on the microwave. "Alright Bryce, you ready?"

He's got his game face on and I'm worried about what that means for me. "Dare," I say, feeling unusually free.

He takes a deep breath before speaking. "I dare you to take a walk with me to the mailbox."

My stomach drops. *Oh, hell no.* I glare back at him. He just took all the fun out of the game. I may be drunk, but I'm not stupid. I down the shot in less than three seconds then scoot my chair out and walk out of the room.

"Bryce!" I hear him calling after me. I can hear his footsteps behind me and then his hand grabbing my arm. "Bryce, where are you going?"

"I've had enough of this stupid game," I reply, a bitter look taking over my face.

We are standing in the hallway. He's managed to stop me from walking away. He is standing in front of me and I can't even look him in the eyes.

"Bryce, I'm sorry," he stammers. "I didn't mean to upset you. Just come back to the table and…"

"No!" I shove him roughly. More rough than I probably should have, anger is building up inside me. "You just had to take it there…didn't you? Was that your plan all along? Get me drunk and convince me to forget everything?"

"I don't know what I was thinking. I'm sorry. Please, Bryce, I didn't mean to upset you. It's just the alcohol talking." I can see him shove his hands in his pockets awkwardly.

I'm furious with him. Tyson of all people. *He should have known better.*

He reaches his hand up so that his fingers grace my chin, tilting it upward. I am now finally looking him in the eyes. My skin feels hot beneath his touch. I avert his gaze, but he follows it with his body.

"Bryce, please, just look at me," he pleads. Against my better judgment, I do exactly as he asks. When our eyes finally lock, he sighs loudly. "You know I would never let anyone hurt you, right?"

His words are so sincere, so genuine. This is the first time I've ever been upset with Tyson and I feel more disappointed in myself.

I look down at my feet, and again he tilts my chin back up so we are staring into one another's eyes. There is something about the way he looks at me, like he can see through to my soul. It makes me shudder. Not in a bad way, but in a way I've never felt before. My tongue is dry, and I'm swallowing madly.

Best friends shouldn't feel this way. Something has shifted, and I'm not sure I'm ready to confront the change just yet. The tension is high and thick.

"Bryce," he says my name softly, and then he begins inching closer.

My mind goes into overdrive and I freak out. *Best friends don't kiss.* My heart is pounding wildly as I rack my brain of how to get out of this predicament without ruining our friendship altogether. "I can't," I stammer as I push him away and run upstairs to the bathroom.

I lock the door and lean against it, my mind and heart at an all-time war. I breathe in deeply, trying to make sense of what just happened…or almost happened. I can't even think clearly. My best friend almost kissed me, and although I pushed him away, I'm pretty sure I wanted it.

Before

* * *

My breathing takes me by surprise, overwhelming and frantic. I'm running for the front entrance as soon as I hear the familiar roar of his engine driving away. I rip open the door, the cool air slapping me in the face, and I keel over, gasping for air.

Robbie hasn't let me leave the house in over a week. He forced me to call in sick to work and took the keys to my car. This is the first time he's let me out of his sight. It's only because he doesn't have any more sick days at his job, so he had to go in. I've been waiting for this moment for what seems like an eternity. He can't keep me a prisoner here any longer.

I take a few shaky steps onto the porch and then plop down on the stairs, throwing my head between my knees. He took my phone from me, so I can't call anyone. He's even gone as far as to disable the internet. He'll die before he ever lets me leave.

"Hey there, neighbor!" A familiar voice breaks into my thoughts. I lift my head up and my eyes meet Tyson's. He is wearing a black t-shirt with some band I've never heard of before on it and blue jeans. His dark eyes are warm and inviting.

I force a fake smile upon my lips. "Hey, how's it

going?"

"Whoa," he says, his face falling and concern lacing his tone. "Are you okay?"

I shift my eyes away from him, startled. Shit. *I've been locked up inside for so long, I forgot what my face might look like to the rest of the world. I am sporting a gnarly black eye and a busted lip. "Oh, yeah," I lie, my lip quivering. "I'm such a klutz."*

Tyson continues to eye me down suspiciously. It all happens so quickly: he reaches out to touch my face, and I flinch so severely, he snaps his hand back. It's not you, I want to tell him. How fucked up is it that my first instinct is to pull away, duck, or flinch? "I'm sorry," he stammers. "That was impolite of me."

I look up into his eyes and I can feel the emotions beginning to overtake me. My eyesight is growing blurry, and I'm breathing deeply. "You have nothing to apologize for," I say, my voice quivering.

Tyson takes a seat next to me on the steps, but keeps a good distance. "Look, I know we don't know each other very well, but I want you to know that I'm here for you if you ever need to talk." Besides borrowing eggs and flour a couple of times, we haven't spent more than a total of thirty minutes together since we first met.

I nod, sniffling.

His eyes grow serious. "Whether you got that from being accident prone, or from another reason entirely, you have nothing to be ashamed of, okay?"

I nod, biting my lip. His words help comfort me. I am embarrassed about my injured face. A light bulb goes off inside my head, and my eyes shift over to where his classic dark blue Volkswagen Bug sits in the driveway next door. "Hey, this is going to seem really off the wall, and you can totally say no, please don't feel like I'm pressuring you or anything...but..."

Tyson grows impatient, waiting for me to ask my question. "What do you need, Bryce?"

I lock eyes with him, exhaling sharply. "Do you think you might be able to give me a ride somewhere in a couple of hours?"

His eyes flick to my car. "What happened to your car?" he asks.

I shrug nonchalantly. "It's been giving me problems lately."

He nods, his eyes still focused on my Honda. "No problem. I can take a look at it if you'd like me to," he offers like the gentleman he is.

I shake my head back and forth quickly. "No, it's okay, Robbie is going to take it in," I lie.

Tyson breaks his gaze with my car. "Should I even ask what happened to the window?"

It's too complicated to tell him the truth. I can't get him involved. All I need is a ride, no strings attached.

"What time do you need me here?" he asks.

I glance at the watch on his wrist. 4:23 p.m. Robbie shouldn't be home until well after ten. "Can you meet me here at 6:15?"

He nods with a small smile. "Can do."

"Thanks, Tyson," I reply, jumping up from my seated position and throwing my arms around him. I surprise even myself with the quick movement. Tyson chuckles as I feel his hands lightly graze my back, sending chills up and down my spine. I pull away slowly, my gaze meeting his. It's crazy how right it feels being in his arms. Before I even realize what I am doing, I find myself leaning in to him.

"Whoa," Tyson says softly, pulling away from me. "I am so sorry if I gave you the wrong impression," he says, his face full of sympathy.

My stomach drops as I realize just how badly I've messed up.

Please don't leave me here with him.

I swallow before speaking. "I'm sorry. I—I—I don't even know what I'm doing anymore."

Tyson stares back at me sadly. "Hey, don't even sweat it. Look, you're sexy as hell, but you're not single, and I just met someone."

I don't know why his words cut so deeply. I have no reason to be upset by what he's said, but my mind thinks otherwise. "I hope I can still count on you for that ride. I promise I won't try to kiss you again," I say hoping to lighten the mood.

Tyson cracks a smile. "Of course. I'll be back." He turns his back to me and begins walking the short distance back to his own house.

What the hell are you doing, Bryce? Did you really just try to kiss a neighbor? *I climb back up the porch stairs and back into the house, closing the door behind me.*

I have no time to dwell on what just transpired. Tonight is the night. I'm getting the hell out of here.

Five: Breaking Down the Boundaries

I wake up feeling groggy and slightly hung over. I have a migraine, and the sun is sneaking its way through my blinds and illuminating my small room.

Tyson tried to kiss me last night.

I almost let him.

It's Saturday morning, and I still have a day and a half left with my best friend before my parents' return. That is if he didn't take off already. I wouldn't blame him after our awkward encounter last night.

I toss my comforter off my body and quickly give myself a once over in my vanity mirror. I have bed head, but not terribly bad. I run my fingers through my short hair to attempt to give it some composure. I look down at my oversized shirt and sweatpants before deciding against changing. Tyson has seen me in my pajamas more times than I can count, and I'm too worried that he's upset with me to waste any more time.

Slowly, I pull my door open, trying not to make

too much noise. Last night I gave him permission to sleep in Mikey's room, but when I see Mikey's bed untouched, I know there is something wrong. I race down the stairs, my heartbeat pounding in my ears, and dash to the window inside the study; the one that faces the street. I pull back the blinds and breathe out a sigh of relief when I see Tyson's old beat up Bug in the driveway. *So, he didn't leave.*

I make my way to the living room and sure enough, he is passed out on the couch, hugging the near empty bottle of vodka. I can't help stifling a laugh. He stirs from the noise, tiredly opening his eyes and looking up at me. He must have forgotten what he was holding because the bottle rolls right out of his arms and onto the ground with a thud. I burst out laughing, thankful for the change in the air.

His eyes are only halfway open, but his face holds a confused expression. "What's so funny?" He begins rubbing his eyes.

"You." I continue giggling, then take a seat on the loveseat across from him. "Look, are we okay?" I figure it's better to nip it in the bud then to let it fester any longer.

"Of course, why wouldn't we be?" he asks.

"You don't remember?" There's no way…he definitely wasn't *that* drunk…or was he?

"Remember what?" he asks, sitting up.

I shake my head, frustrated. "Nothing…I guess."

"No, seriously," he presses. "What did I do?"

I can't help but break out into a small grin. "What makes you think that *you* did anything wrong?"

"Because I slept on the couch…I must have been in the doghouse." He shoots a smile back at me.

"Really, it's nothing." If he doesn't remember, then I don't want to refresh his memory. It was awkward enough what transpired last night between us, and I just want things to go back to the way they were—simple.

He shrugs. "What's for breakfast?"

I roll my eyes back at him. "What do I look like? Your chef? Get your ass off the couch and come see the options for yourself."

He breaks out into a wide grin. "There's the Bryce I love."

The minute the words leave his mouth, my cheeks start burning up with a vengeance. Did he just say what I think he did? He couldn't have meant it...I try to dismiss the butterflies that are now swarming in my stomach, making me feel uneasy.

Tyson doesn't seem to be affected whatsoever like I am, as he stands and begins making his way to the kitchen. When he notices I'm not in tow with him, he turns around, locking eyes with me. "You coming?"

"Yeah, right behind you."

Get it together, Bryce.

*   *   *

I'm used to being locked up indoors twenty-four hours a day. Tyson on the other hand? He is basically going stir-crazy. I don't blame him. No one likes to be restricted. He's already left the house three different times. The first time, he went for a run. The second time he went to the grocery store to get us more snacks. And now? He's gone yet again in an attempt at renting us a few Redbox movies to keep us occupied.

It's eight at night and because it is nearing the end of fall, the sun doesn't stay out past seven.

Because it is so dark for the early hour, it's deceiving, and I assume it's later than it actually is.

Tyson left over twenty minutes ago, and with the nearest Redbox less than a couple of blocks away, he should be back any minute. A loud bang catches my attention along with my heart. It is beating so rapidly, I am having trouble breathing.

What was that?

It sounded similar to the loud commotion from the other night. I'm shaking as I peek out the window in the study. It's difficult to make anything out with the sun gone, but for one split second I swear I see someone looking back at me from across the street. I squint my eyes in an attempt to get a better look, but nothing is there.

Still jittery and scared, I pull out my phone and text Tyson. *Are you almost back?*

I honestly don't know what I saw outside the window, but the idea that something or someone is out there is enough to have me double and triple-checking every door and window in the house, making sure they are closed and locked.

Yeah, around the corner. My phone lights up to alert me of his response.

I begin to calm down, but just as I go to close the blinds in my bedroom, I see something again. This time I am positive it is a silhouette of a person. A man. I can't see much, but all hairs on the back of my neck stand up when the hooded figure looks up to where I am standing. I jump back from the window, shakily dialing 911, when I hear the front door open and close again.

I'm so frightened, that I instantly climb inside my closet, crouching down so that I am hidden behind my clothes. I am shaking something fierce as I hear the audible footsteps downstairs and then as they begin to ascend the stairs. I am clutching my phone to my chest tightly, 911 already keyed in, ready to press dial at any minute when I hear *his* familiar voice.

"Bryce?"

I close my eyes and let out a sigh of relief. *It's just Tyson.* I'm beginning to feel like a lunatic as I make my way out of my closet, trying to be stealthy. It doesn't work so well, he is standing in my doorway when I slide open the door and walk out.

"Bryce?" he asks again, a confused, yet concerned look overtaking his face. "Are you okay?"

I am beyond mortified. "Yeah, yeah," I stutter, running my fingers through my hair and shoving my phone into the pocket of my jeans.

"What were you doing in the closet?" he questions, inching toward me.

"Nothing." I want to be better at lying, but I am still shaken up about what I think I saw. I also know how crazy I look, and I don't want to scare Tyson off.

He is now directly in front of me, looking down, straight into my eyes. "You can tell me anything."

My heart is doing summersaults. Partly because it's still not fully recovered, and partly because he is standing so close I can feel his warm breath on my cheek.

"I think I saw something…or someone, outside." I barely get out in an audible sentence.

"What?" He rushes past me and to my window, pulling the blinds back and peering out. "Where? What did you see?"

Okay…so he doesn't think I'm crazy.

I walk up behind him. "I thought I saw someone outside across the street. When I looked out the window earlier, I could have sworn someone was out there, watching me."

Tyson brushes past me so quickly, it startles me. "Where are you going?" I exclaim as I follow him down the stairs. He is barreling down them, taking two at a time, and headed straight for the front door.

"Tyson!" I cry out, attempting to get his attention. "What are you doing?"

"I'm going to see if anyone is out there." He begins to fiddle with the lock on the front door, when I stop him.

"No! Please, I don't want to be left alone," I beg.

Tyson turns to look at me, taking my face in his hands gently. "I promise I won't let anything happen to you but I have to check it out. Lock the door behind me."

"But…"

"No buts," he cuts me off. He lets his hands drop from my face, but I can still feel the heat lingering from his touch. "I promise, I will be right back. Watch out the window for me, and I will signal when I want you to open back up." He flips on the front porch light before slipping out the door.

I quickly lock both the handle and deadbolt and rush to the window, peering outside. It's dark, but with the porch light on, I can see quite a good portion of the front yard and driveway. I watch as Tyson slinks around the house, cautiously looking for anything out of the ordinary. I lose sight of him when he runs across the street, but see his silhouette illuminated under one of the dim lamp posts.

My heart is beating in my ear; the suspense killing me. After a few moments I see him jog back over to the front of the house, but instead of heading for the door, he ends up veering off towards the right side of the house. I lose track of him, but hear a huge thud and then bang and my body instantly takes over. I am racing to the door before I have time to process a thought of what is happening.

"Mother fucker!" I hear Tyson exclaim loudly, and I bolt out the door in the direction of his voice.

"Tyson! Tyson!" I scream, my feet not moving fast enough.

As I make it around the side of my house, I see what looks to be our garbage can tipped over, spilled out all over the ground, and Tyson in the midst of it.

"Tyson! Are you okay?" I rush to his side, helping him stand.

There is a look of shock playing across his eyes, and his jaw is hanging wide open. "Bryce?" he asks.

"Are you okay? What happened?" My heart is still piercing my ears, but I have to make sure he isn't injured. I have to make sure the man I saw from earlier didn't hurt him.

He nods slowly. "Bryce…" he pauses, still appearing in shock. "You did it."

Did what? Confusion is bubbling up inside me, and then a gust of wind sends goose bumps throughout my body, and I understand what he is referring to.

This is the first time I've been outside in over a year. My eyes are darting around the yard and neighborhood quickly. "*Holy* shit." My hand flies up to cover my mouth.

"What…what…why?" Tyson, still in shock, can't even form full sentences.

"I heard a loud noise, and I thought you were hurt."

"I tripped over the garbage can. You really thought I was in trouble?" His eyes are big and wide, trying to piece together how I overcame my debilitating fear.

I nod. "I'm outside." The revelation finally hits me as tears begin to well up in my eyes. I am staring up into the sky, breathing in the fresh air, and I've never felt more alive.

Tyson pulls me into him, wrapping his arms around my body tightly. "You did it…you really did it."

I smile proudly. "I did it."

Tyson releases me. "Remember after the accident, when you were in the hospital?"

I nod. It feels like an eternity ago.

"I can still remember the way you flinched at any noise, quiet or loud. You had reoccurring nightmares almost every night, and you barely spoke." I continue nodding, wondering what point he is getting at. "I used to have one-sided conversations with you."

I bob my head in agreement. "I remember."

He runs his hand through his hair. "You've come so far since then."

I think back on the broken girl I used to be. I couldn't even look at myself in a mirror. I wanted so badly to give up…but Tyson and my family refused to give up on me. They reminded me that everything happens for a reason and that I survived because I was a warrior. "I couldn't have done it without you."

Tyson pulls my head against his chest. "You don't give yourself enough credit." I will never tire of his intoxicating smell. I close my eyes, breathing in deeply.

We stay out there for another twenty minutes, basking in my victory.

I faced my fear, and I came out unscathed. It's the most empowering feeling in the entire world.

Before

* * *

Something is terribly wrong.

My legs feel like jello as I run quickly to the window that overlooks our driveway. My stomach plummets, making me gag. Robbie's red Ford pick-up pulls onto the dark pavement. My eyes dart back to the clock on my nightstand. 5:27. I don't know what he is doing home, but I know if he finds me like this, I'm in trouble. I scoop up all the items scattered atop our bed and throw them into the big duffle bag which is lying at my feet. Once they are secure inside, I zip it up quickly and throw it under the bed.

I'm shaking uncontrollably, when I hear the front door slam and his loud footsteps downstairs.

You're not supposed to be home. You're not supposed to be home.

My heart is beating rapidly, and my eyes are darting around the room nervously. He is barreling up the stairs loudly, and I quickly throw myself onto the bed, grabbing a book off my nightstand. I lie back against the pillows and focus my eyes onto the page in front of me.

I see him outside the door from my peripherals, the

beating of my heart steadily increasing. I can't even focus. The words look blurry to me, I'm blinded by my fear. His fingers reach for my book, pulling it from my hands and throwing it on the ground. He kicks off his boots and then climbs onto the bed, pushing me to the middle.

Just act normal. He won't know a thing.

He reaches over, pulling me into him. "You haven't even asked me how my day was," he whispers against my mouth.

He reeks of alcohol, it smells like he bathed in it.

"Have you been drinking?" I ask the obvious question.

Robbie wiggles his finger back and forth in front of my face. "Ask me."

I sigh, giving in. "How was your day?" I don't even recognize my own voice.

"Terrible. I hate spending time away from you." He moves his lips across my neck. "What did you do all day?"

I shake my head. "Just cleaned up a bit and read. I'm not feeling good."

He pulls away, his eyes locking with mine. He lifts the back of his hand up, pressing it against my forehead.

"You're not running a fever."

"Not that kind of sick, I just have a stomach ache." I'm hoping he won't want to get hot and heavy with me if he thinks I have an upset stomach. I've been avoiding sex with him for weeks now. Luckily, he hasn't caught on yet. I've been able to convince him that I've been on my period and haven't felt well since.

Robbie groans and then rolls away from me. He lowers one of his feet to the floor, and then I see his body go crashing down.

"Babe?" I cry out, surprised. I crawl to the edge of the bed and the handle of the duffle bag is wrapped around his ankle. My stomach tenses up immediately. He rips it away from his body and then glares back at me. As he stands, he places the bag onto the bed slowly, keeping his eyes trained on me. He begins unzipping it, the suspense killing me. He reaches into the bag pulling out my clothes and toiletries.

"What is this?" he asks in an unusually soft tone.

"Nothing," I try to sound convincing.

"Why the fuck is there a packed bag hidden under our bed?" he bellows loudly straight into my face.

I'm shaking in terror, just shaking my head back and forth. He drops my personal belongings onto the bed and grabs my wrists pulling me up roughly. His nose is pressed up against mine and his expression is hard. "You little slut," he hisses under his breath. "I should have known you would leave me the minute after you spread your legs."

His words use to hurt like the deepest cuts, but I'm numb to them now. I'm a whore, a slut, a waste of space. I'm a worthless piece of shit, and I deserve to die. I've heard it all. I avoid eye contact, tipping my face away from his.

"Let me go," I bite out through a tight jaw.

Robbie doesn't move an inch. "If I can't have you, no one can." His words come out in a threat. I don't even see his elbow until it's too late, it collides with my right eye, and I'm down for the count.

Six: Returning to the Scene of the Crime

One step.

One step was all it took to begin to put my life back on track.

One step was all that was holding me back from everything I had ever been—everything I could ever become.

Once I faced my fear head on and came out on top, it was as though all of my inhibitions about leaving the house simply faded away.

Tyson and I spent Sunday morning walking around my entire neighborhood for hours. We could go anywhere, do anything, but he was afraid of pushing me too far, too fast. I was just excited to be able to feel normal for the first time in what felt like forever. I wasn't confined to the house I had grown up in.

When my parents came home and I greeted them from the front porch, my mother broke down; cried like I've never seen before. Then she began thanking God that a miracle happened. I had to tell her it wasn't God that made it happen, it was all me. I had it inside me all along…I just needed a little push.

It's Tuesday evening and now that I don't feel like a prisoner anymore, I want to get out and simply do something. I pull out my phone and call Tyson. He's the only person I can think of celebrating with. He's the only person I *want* to be celebrating with. When he doesn't answer, I don't let it stop me. For the first time in over a year, I take care in picking out what I will wear. I pull out one of my favorite dresses; it is black and white, with small polka dots on top and large ones on the bottom. It is sleeveless and I pair it with my favorite thick black belt, tights, and cardigan. I haven't had a reason to wear heels, but tonight is reason enough, so I slip on my black studded heels and give myself a once over in my full-length mirror.

Not half bad.

I don't wear any make-up other than eyeliner, mascara, and blush. I've always considered myself lucky that it takes me only fifteen minutes if I don't need to shower. High-maintenance and I don't mix, and I am thankful for that.

I pass the living room where my parents are seated in their usual spots watching television. "Bryce, is that you?" My mother calls out when she hears the tapping of my heels.

I pop my head in and notice Mikey is also in the room, deeply lost in his Gameboy. He doesn't even bother looking up.

"Oh my gosh!" my mother gushes when she sees me, her hands going straight to her mouth. "You look beautiful!"

This warrants Mikey's attention as he curiously looks up from his game's small screen.

"Doesn't she look beautiful, Tom?" my mother exclaims.

He nods smiling back at me. "You look beautiful, Bryce. You headed somewhere?"

I shrug. "I don't know. I just felt like dressing up. I can't get ahold of Tyson, but I think I am going to go downtown anyways."

I've never seen my parents smile bigger.

My mother instantly stands and rushes to me, embracing me tightly. "Have I told you how proud I am of you?"

I can't help but smile. I'm proud of me too. A couple of days ago this would be my worst nightmare; but not today. Today, I couldn't be more excited for what lies ahead. I nod into her shoulder.

She releases me, but still holds one of my hands. "We all are."

I blush. I've been waiting a long time to hear my parents say anything like that. "Thanks," I say sheepishly.

"Now go out and paint the town red!" my mother exclaims with a wide-eyed expression.

I nod and then make my way out to the garage where my car has been sitting untouched. As I climb in the driver's seat, I let my fingers slide across the dashboard and steering wheel. *Just like riding a bike.*

I pull out my cell phone from my purse and attempt to call Tyson once more before I make my way into downtown Phoenix all by myself. This time he answers.

"Hello?" he says, but something is different in his voice.

"Tyson?"

"Hey," he replies, sounding strange, almost as if he is out of breath.

"Are you okay?" I ask, not sure what is going on.

"Yeah," he says and then groans in pain.

"What's going on?" I ask, my heart beginning to beat frantically.

"I got in a car accident." Weak. He sounds weak.

"What?" I cry out. "Are you okay? Where are you?"

He starts coughing lightly. "I'm at home."

"At home? What do you mean you're at home?" My mind is racing a mile a minute. "I thought you said you got in a car accident?"

"I did," he replies softly. "On Sunday."

"Sunday?" He was with me Sunday. How could he have…? "I'm coming. Don't move!" I hang up the phone quickly. I can't wait any longer. The suspense is killing me. I press the button on the garage door opener and race as quickly as I can down the driveway.

I don't realize it until I've driven nearly the entire way there that I am returning to the scene of the crime. Tyson still lives in the same house that he did when we originally met. I have to see my old house and the exact spot Robbie lit me on fire. I think I'm going to have an anxiety attack.

I debate turning around, but I know Tyson needs me. He needs me to be strong for him. When I arrive and park, I try to avoid letting my eyes glance over to the area, but it's harder than I thought it would be. I can see the spot clear as day. There is no grass there, still, just dirt. It's a terrible reminder. I shudder and then quickly race up the stairs at Tyson's house. I knock frantically at the door, hoping they won't leave me out staring at my past for too long.

One of Tyson's roommates opens the door. He is freakishly tall, dark skinned, and lanky.

"I'm here to see Tyson," I greet him.

"Sure, come on in." He opens the door wide for me to enter and then closes it behind me. "You must be Bryce."

"You've heard about me?" I ask, shaking his gigantic hand.

"Heard about you?" He laughs heartily. "Tyson hasn't shut up about you since I moved in. I've been wondering when I would meet you."

"And you are?" He obviously has spoken to Tyson about me, but strangely, Tyson doesn't speak about his roommates often.

"I'm Grae."

"Nice to meet you." I avert my eyes from his and look down the hall, perplexed.

"His bedroom is normally upstairs, but because of the accident, I've been letting him use my bed. Come on, I'll show you where it is." He reads my mind with little to no effort.

"Is he okay?" I ask as I anxiously follow his tall frame down the hall.

"He will be."

I let those words consume me as he finally rounds the last corner and opens a red door. Behind it, I can see Tyson lying on the bed. I don't see any casts of any sort, so that has to be a good sign.

Tyson gazes up, appearing tired. "I can't believe you…"

His face is cut and bruised in multiple places. His lip looks busted open.

I rush past Grae and straight to his bed. "What happened?" I sit down gently beside Tyson, careful not to get too close as I still have no clue how serious his injuries are.

"I don't know." He shakes his head lightly. "I remember leaving your house, and then you know the stoplight on Jefferson and Third?"

I nod.

"It was a yellow light and I was a decent amount away, so I tried braking, and nothing. My brakes were completely out. My car went through the red light, and I got sideswiped."

"What do you mean your brakes were out?" I press, wanting to know more.

"I mean, I was pressing it and nothing was happening…they think someone tampered with them."

I gasp. "What? Are you serious?"

"The cop on the scene checked my brake line and told me later that it was cut."

I swallow, trying to digest the information he is feeding me without completely breaking down.

"Who would do something so malicious like that?" I ask. "Wasn't your car fine when you went to get the movies on Saturday night?"

He nods. "It was working fine, which means it had to have happened between Saturday night and Sunday afternoon."

I think back to that timeframe and suddenly, a chill takes over my entire body. "No." I shake my head profusely.

"What is it?" he asks, his chocolate eyes boring into mine.

"It can't be." I stand up quickly from the bed and begin pacing.

He is watching me intently with his eyes and attempts to sit up further, then cries out in pain.

I rush to his side. "You alright?"

He fights to smile. "Yeah, just dealing with a few broken ribs, a concussion, and a lot of cuts and bruises." His expression hardens. "Now tell me what you were about to say."

I take a deep breath in, trying to contemplate the possibility of what is about to come out of my mouth. "Remember the other night at my house when I told you I thought I saw someone outside?"

He nods, fixated on me.

"What do you think the chances are that person is the same person who cut your brake line?"

He sighs loudly, running his hand over his hair. "A definite possibility."

I shudder at the thoughts racing through my mind. "What if that person was Robbie?"

Tyson's eyes bulge out at me. "Robbie...*your* Robbie?"

I nod.

"Then I think we need to make a police report."

I swallow, digesting everything. "You didn't make one already?"

He shakes his head. "They did a report on my accident and then called me to let me know about the brake line being cut. They asked me if I had any idea of anyone who would want to harm me. At the time, I couldn't think of anyone."

I take a deep breath in, attempting to slow my dizzying thoughts. "What if it *is* Robbie?" I can't help the fear that radiates off of my voice.

Tyson grabs my hand quickly, giving it a reassuring squeeze. "Then he's going to be sorry. I won't let anything happen to you. I promise."

I shoot him a small smile back. He could have died and yet, I'm still the one he wants to protect after it all. I don't know that I deserve him, but I definitely appreciate him.

Before

*   *   *

"I haven't accepted my body fully yet, but it's getting easier to think about it."

"Thank you, Eileen," Jerry initiates the clapping. "Who's next?" His emerald eyes scan the small circle and I keep mine trained to the ground. If I don't make eye contact, he won't call on me.

I've been attending a support group at the hospital. It's all burn victims and it's supposed to be a way to help us overcome our hesitations out in the real world and with our own body image. I don't even recognize the skin I'm in anymore. It's littered with discolored scars even after the three surgeries I've already endured. I'm scheduled for another surgery in a few weeks, but I am beginning to lose faith that I will ever get back to the girl I used to be. I feel like an imposter in her skin.

The depression has been unbearable most days so I've been keeping to myself. Turns out, it's been a lot easier to play pretend. To shut myself down, not speak with anyone, and daydream about the alternate route my life could have taken. They say I'm almost ready to leave here. I can't go back to my old house, so my parents have offered to take me back in. I don't want to burden them, but it does make me feel safer knowing I won't be alone. My mother's been begging me to talk to her for weeks now, but I have no energy. It's hard enough to keep my eyelids open, much less hold any sort of conversation.

She's worried about me; about what I might do. I've heard her speak to my nurses, asking if my behavior is normal. I don't even know what normal is anymore. Robbie is still out there. For all I know, he's going to be back to finish the job. I have nightmares about it nightly, sweating out my fears.

The police have been hunting for Robbie since the night he tried to take my life from me. There are leads every day pertaining to his whereabouts, but it's as if he vanished without a trace. Sometimes I'm too scared to sleep. My anxiety gets the better of me most nights. I used to be somebody, now I feel invisible, like a nobody. No one is ever going to want me now.

"Okay, guys, thanks for the great day today. We're done. I'll see you guys back here on Tuesday," Jerry's voice breaks into my thoughts. I blink my eyes a few times, surprised the group is over.

I'm leaving here in a couple of days, they've been hinting at it all week. I'm panicking. At the hospital, there are people around constantly so I never feel like I'm alone. My parents have their own lives so I know they aren't going to be able to stay home with me all the time. I feel crippled by fear. He took away everything from me: my dignity, my physical appearance, my confidence. He doesn't deserve another thought from me, but I'm worried I am never going to be free of my fear as long as he is still out there.

Seven: That Time My Best Friend Confessed His Feelings for Me

A few days later after Tyson has had a chance to rest up, we make our way into the police station to file a report on the man we saw outside my window, and the brake line issue with Tyson's car. Because we have no firm proof, I'm not sure how much good it will do, but it does make me feel more secure.

As we exit the courthouse, a bubbly blond comes bouncing up the stairs, nearly running me over. "Um, excuse me," I say shortly as her shoulder comes into contact with mine.

"Oh, I'm sorry," she says, and then her eyes lock on Tyson's. "Tyson! I heard about your accident, are you okay?" She forgets I exist as she quickly shuffles over to him and gives him a hug.

"Ouch," he mutters from the impact.

"I'm sorry!" Her apology to him seems more sincere. "Are you okay?"

He breaks out into a smile. "Yeah, just a few fractured ribs. How have you been?"

What the hell? It's not like I'm standing here or anything.

"I've been good! Just here to pay off a traffic ticket." She giggles like she just said something funny.

I clear my throat obnoxiously hoping Tyson will catch on.

"Oh yeah," he says, slapping himself on the forehead. "I'm sorry, I forgot to introduce you. Ashleigh, this is Bryce. Bryce, Ashleigh."

I don't know why, but it really irritates me that he leads with her name. I've never heard of her before and I *am* his best friend.

She smiles brightly my way. "What an interesting name."

"You've never met anyone named Bryce before?" I ask, highly doubting it.

"Oh, I definitely have…just never met a girl named Bryce before." I feel like she is taking a stab at me somehow.

"Well now you have," I reply stiffly. I want Tyson to finish chatting her up so we can be on our merry way.

She shifts her attention back to him. "You know, I haven't seen you since…" she trails off, sliding a finger down his chest. *Don't mind me, I'm not really here.* I just want to disappear.

He nods and for the first time in my life, I swear I see Tyson blush. "Yeah," he responds, rubbing the back of his hair. "I'm sorry about that."

She shrugs, a smile pulling at her lips. "Maybe when you're all healed we can hang out or something?"

Irritation is bubbling inside me. *Since when?* I'm not really keen on them hanging out *again*. I'm anxious to know about their history.

He grins. "Yeah, I'd like that."

"Me too." She shuffles around in her purse, pulling out a piece of gum and popping it into her mouth. "Well you know where to find me. I better get going. Nice to meet you, *Bryce*." It takes everything in me not to lunge for her throat.

"What was that all about?" I ask Tyson the minute she is out of earshot.

"What?" he replies, innocently.

"*That.*" I glance back at her.

"Oh," he says, pausing. "I met Ashleigh at a party in the dorms."

"How many times have you two hung out?" I ask.

Tyson sighs, rubbing his hand over his arm. "I don't know, two or three times, maybe."

I nod, irritated. "Did you hook-up with her?"

His eyes widen, surprised. "Maybe. Since when do you care?"

His question is like a stab to the heart. *Since forever...? I thought we told each other everything? How much have you left unsaid?*

"I don't," I recover quickly. "I just can't picture you with a girl like *that*."

Tyson stops walking abruptly, and looks me straight in the eye. "Hold up, what's wrong with Ashleigh?"

My cheeks instantly begin burning up. I'm starting to think I don't know Tyson as well as I thought I did.

"Nothing." I decide to drop it. I'm already

irritated beyond belief and just want to go home.

"No." He throws an arm in front of me to stop me from walking away. "Are you jealous?"

Jealous? Why in the world would I ever be jealous? I shake my head. "No."

"Good, because I don't want to have to remind you that we aren't dating." He motions between the two of us. "What I do or don't do with my love life is completely my business."

I feel a pang in my chest when he refers to his love life. "Fine," I reply shortly, turning on my heel and heading back to the car. I can feel the tears stinging the edges of my eyes, but he won't get the satisfaction of seeing me cry today.

* * *

Things have been strange with Tyson since a few days ago; the day at the courthouse. He was short with me, and I didn't like it. Although it's been difficult, I've abstained from calling or texting him. I feel like he owes me an apology, but I'm not quite sure he sees it that way.

I've been more cautious when coming and going, but for the most part, I am finally beginning to feel an ounce of normal. I don't have panic attacks when I'm outside anymore. It feels amazing to feel regular. I've taken the liberty of scheduling myself a few interviews for jobs. My parents are ecstatic. Even Mikey is smiling more. I think they are excited about the possibility of getting me out of their hair once and for all.

I have an interview today for a receptionist position at a local hair salon. It's nothing huge or fancy, but I have butterflies just thinking about it. I hope I will make a good impression. I hope I will fit in.

After dressing in a nice long-sleeve blouse and black pants, I make my way to the salon, a few miles down the road. There are about eight stations along with a nail salon as well. It's a higher end beauty salon, and it reeks of sophistication.

An older lady in her late fifties approaches me. She has honey blond hair and blue eyes. She lets her eyes trail up and down my body. "Let me guess, Bryce?"

I nod, smiling. "You got me."

She smiles lazily. "Well, come on down, I'll get Janet."

I follow her down through the rows of stations, eyes falling on me from both sides of the room. She opens a door in the back and it leads to a small office. There is a woman, short dark hair and brown eyes, probably in her mid-thirties, mulling over a heap of paperwork.

"Hi, you must be Bryce," she greets me warmly before we are left alone and the door is closed behind me. "Go ahead, take a seat."

"Thank you," I reply, following her instructions.

She is wearing glasses that are positioned on the bridge of her nose, which she lifts off and sets down on the desk in front of her. "Do you have your resume?"

I nod, reaching into my purse to pull out a creased copy. "I hope this is okay. I didn't want it to get wet." It was sprinkling when I arrived, so to protect my resume, I ended up stuffing it in my purse.

She shakes her head yes before grabbing it out of my hand. "Oh yes, now I remember. So it looks like you worked at Forever 21, Olive Garden, Tan Republic, and went to school. Although, I don't see anything listed here for the last year. What have you been up to?"

My chest tightens. It's hard enough that I have to live with it, but having to explain it to someone else? It always worries me that they won't be as understanding as my family has been.

"There was an accident, and I was healing for most of that time."

She puts my resume down, squinting her eyes at me. "Oh my, well I hope everything is better now."

My heart begins thudding against my chest.

I swallow loudly, nodding.

She breathes deeply. "Well, what makes you want to work here?"

I smile gently. "I like customer service. I enjoy putting a smile on people's faces."

We talk for another twenty minutes, and after she drills me, she takes me on a tour of the building.

"Look," she says as I stand by the entrance at the end of the tour. "I don't normally do this, but I have a gut feeling about you. I'd like to offer you the job."

I gasp, surprised. "Seriously?"

She smiles, her eyes lighting up. "Yeah, I think you'll fit in just great here."

I can't help returning her wide smile. "Thank you so much. Can I ask you about wardrobe?"

She looks at what I am wearing. "This is perfect."

I blow out a sigh of relief. "Great."

"Why don't you come back here on Monday at 9:00 a.m. and we'll get you training?"

I giggle. "I'll be here."

I walk out of the salon feeling high on life. *It wasn't as bad as you thought it would be.*

I can't wait to share the good news with my family and Tyson. I hope he's gotten over being a douche, because I know he'll be excited for me.

After climbing into my car, I hit my speed dial, anxiety pouring out of me.

A few rings in, a high-pitched female voice answers. "Tyson's phone."

My heart goes into overdrive. It's not familiar to me, but if I could take a guess, I'd say it's Ashleigh the bimbo. I gulp before responding, making sure to check myself. "Um, is Tyson there?"

"Who's calling?" she asks in a rather annoyed fashion.

"Bryce."

I can almost feel her rolling her eyes from the other side of the phone. "Tyson, Bryce is on the phone." She sounds muffled as she relays the message. No more than a few seconds later, I hear Tyson's familiar voice.

"Hey, what's up?" He doesn't sound as welcoming as normal, and I know it probably has to do with how we left things.

"Hey," I say, unsure of how to proceed. "I haven't heard from you in a few days, and I just wanted to see if you might want to hang out?"

He sighs. "Tonight isn't a good night, Bryce. Is everything okay with you?" Although he turns down my offer, he still cares enough to ask how I'm doing, which I appreciate.

"Oh, okay…I guess I'll just talk to you later then," I reply, dejected.

"Bryce," he says, without an immediate follow-up.

"I get it," I say. "You have company. Don't let me interrupt you." I don't wait to hear his response before hanging up. I was so excited to tell him about my new job…but the bimbo who answered his phone ruined it for me.

There is a sharp pain in my chest, and I breathe in deeply, attempting to keep the tears at bay. It's times like this where having more than one friend would really come in handy. I think about heading straight home, but that would just be cowardly. I wanted to celebrate my new position with Tyson, but that obviously isn't going to happen. That doesn't mean I can't celebrate it on my own. I start my car and begin making my way downtown.

* * *

"What can I get you, darlin'?" The bartender at Side Bar asks. He has a rockabilly look with semi-long slicked back light brown hair, sleeves of tattoos, and the most impressive mustache. It's one that is twirled on the ends, and I'm sure he takes wax to on a daily basis. He wears a kind expression and has a gentle demeanor that instantly puts me at ease.

"Can I have a Seven and Seven?" I ask.

He nods and pushes off the bar, beginning to make my drink almost immediately. My eyes scan the room, which is decently filled with other patrons. It's a Thursday night, and I'm surprised to see that I'm not the only one who had the idea to come here. There is a group of ten or so people occupying two tables, which they have pushed together and they are loud and rambunctious. It looks to be a bridal party of some sort as one of the females is wearing a white veil on the top of her head. There is an older couple in their mid-to-late forties beside them huddled up in a booth in the corner. Everyone seems to be here with someone, but me. I've never been much of a drinker, much less someone to drink alone, but I'm taking advantage of my new found freedom.

I see the bartender slide the drink across the bar, which lands directly in front of me. I break my gaze from people-watching and shift my eyes to his. "Would you like to pay or open a tab?"

I think about it for a second before responding, "Why don't you open me a tab?"

He nods smiling back at me. "Waiting on someone?"

My cheeks grow hotter. "Nope, just me."

He gives me the once over, nodding slowly. "Alright then." He spins around headed straight for the cash register. I have no idea if he is judging me or not, but I shouldn't be embarrassed. This is the most fearless thing I've done in a very long time. If anything, tonight should be all about celebrating.

I sip on my drink and twirl back around. I used to love people watching; imagining who certain strangers were and what their lives were like. My eyes land back onto the bridal party and I find myself living vicariously through their boisterous laughter.

The bride-to-be locks eyes with me and her lips curl up into a welcoming smile. I return her smile along with her wave. She excuses herself from her rambunctious group and makes her way right to me. My heart begins thudding in my chest. I'm still not very good with speaking to new people.

"Hey," I hear her high-pitched voice beside me, and then watch her take a seat out of the corner of my eye.

I shift my body toward hers and then meet her gaze. "Hi."

The bartender appears in front of us, placing a napkin in front of my new acquaintance.

"What can I get ya, darlin'?"

She glances at my near empty glass. "I'll have whatever she's having, and get her another one while you're at it."

"Oh, you don't have to..." I hold up my hands in surrender, taken by surprise from her friendly gesture.

"Don't be silly." The beautiful stranger waves her hand in front of my face. Her eye color leaves me speechless...a mixture between sea green and aqua. Her long blonde curls frame her face perfectly and her pink lips are big and plump. "I'm Phoebe." She extends out her hand for me to shake.

"Bryce," I reply, gripping her hand firmly.

"I'm marrying my best friend this weekend," Phoebe says, leaning back in her chair.

"You don't seem overly excited about that." In fact, I could have sworn I heard dread in her voice.

"Don't get me wrong." She sighs. "I love him. I really do, but I'm losing my independence."

I giggle wishing that I had her problems. My life would be a hell of a lot easier. "What gave you that idea?"

The bartender places our drinks in front of us and Phoebe grabs hers, taking a long swig. "I am going to have to consider another person's feelings for the rest of my life. Doesn't that sound dreadful to you?"

I laugh, finishing off my first drink and transferring my straw to the new one. "That sounds like love to me."

Phoebe chuckles, catching the bartender's attention and ordering another drink.

Three drinks in and my cheeks are growing hotter by the minute, my bladder feels like it might explode, and I have somehow managed to find myself smack dab in the middle of the Bachelorette party. When I enter the bathroom, I see the bride-to-be sprawled out on the floor, a tiara on her head, laughing uncontrollably. "Phoebe," I say, reaching out for her shoulder.

She whips her head up to look at me. "Girl!" she wails loudly, reaching her arms up to me, her head flopping back and forth. I grab her hands and pull her up. "I am so happy I met you. Like, I have never felt as close to someone as quickly as I have you." She wraps her arms around me and pulls me into a tight hug. I'm feeling slightly buzzed and a bit nauseous, but like I have a lot of love to give. "I think we need to go back out there and convince them that we met years ago and that we are long, lost friends."

I nod, giggling. "I'm down with that plan, but I need another drink first!"

Phoebe's sea-green eyes drop to my hands. "We *need* to take care of that, pronto! Just follow me, girl. I'm the bride-to-be, I'm like royalty tonight."

It's been so long since I've felt carefree like this. I don't want the feeling to end.

* * *

The loud music and disco lights are causing me to break out into uncontrollable fits of laughter. It's been a long time since I've been in an establishment as classy as this one. I'm trying to remember whose idea this was…but it doesn't even matter. I'm so drunk, I'd agree to the stupidest of plans.

There are three stages with strategically placed stripper poles and people crowded around them. I've lost track of how much I've drank, but the drunk-munchies are taking over me. All I can think of is food. I order a platter and eat almost the entire thing myself.

I can't remember how I got here, but after I finish eating, all I want to do is go home. I'm tired, and the food isn't settling so well inside my stomach. I pull out my cell phone, scrolling down my contact list. "Better not be a douche," I mutter to myself as I press dial on Tyson's number.

After three rings, and when I've almost given up, he picks up. "Hello?" he answers.

"Tyson, thank God you answered!" I say dramatically, speaking with my hands even though he can't see me.

"Bryce, it's late, is everything alright?" he asks frantically.

"Oh, yeah, I'm fine, I'm fine, but listen, can you come pick me up?"

"Why are you whispering?" he replies.

My eyes dart around the strip club I'm at. I'm not sure why. No one is standing near me from the Bachelorette party.

"I don't know. Can you give me a lift or not?" I snap.

There is a long silent pause and I'm positive I've offended him, when he finally answers. "Where are you, Bryce?"

My eyes narrow as I lower my voice. "I'm at Cheetah's."

"You're where?" his voice raises an octave as he questions me.

"You heard me. I'll explain later."

It's not more than twenty minutes later when Tyson pulls up to the front of the dingy strip club. I walk out the door and past the bouncers. "Have a good night," the bigger one addresses me.

"You too," I call out in response and then hop into Tyson's Bug.

As I buckle up, Tyson keeps his eyes trained on me.

"What?" I ask, irritated.

"Seriously?" he chuckles as we drive off.

I don't feel like talking about it with him at all now. We drive in silence for the first ten minutes before it becomes excruciatingly uncomfortable.

"You know, I can't always be your knight in shining armor," Tyson says, his eyes trained on the road.

"I know," I say in a small voice. "Things feel different between us."

He shifts his eyes quickly from the road to me and then back again. "What did you expect?" he asks, shortly.

"What's that supposed to mean?" I press.

"It means that I misread things, and tried to kiss you and you pushed me away." I glance at him quickly, my heart plummeting. *So you did remember...*

"Tyson..." I begin, but am interrupted.

"It's okay, Bryce. I've been looking for that answer for a long time, and you gave it to me." He shuts me down. I can tell he's hurt, and it kills me because I know I am the cause for it.

"It's not that easy," I protest. "Pull the car over."

"Actually, Bryce, it is that easy, and you're almost home, no need to prolong this."

"You're asking for something from me that I can't give to anyone. You're pushing me. I'm not ready. I don't want to lose you, Tyson, but I feel pressured."

"All I'm asking you to do is take a leap of faith. My feelings for you are far deeper than a simple friendship. I lo—"

I can't let him finish. My mind is already finishing his sentence for him, and it's scaring the living hell out of me. "Don't," I say softly. "The minute you cross that line, we can't ever go back. No rewind button. You're my best friend, Tyson. I can't lose you."

Tyson sighs, reaching out the back of his hand and lightly grazing it across my cheek. "Let me show you the kind of love you deserve," he murmurs.

I close my eyes for a brief moment, trying to imagine it. What if we find out we're better off as friends? What if it ruins our bond forever? What if we cross that line and can never go back to the way things were?

"You have been the only person in my life apart from my family, who has been there for me through it all. You know firsthand what I've been through, you were there." I pause, carefully pondering over my next statement.

"If the timing were different, maybe I would be interested in pursuing a deeper connection...but, I still have a lot of problems, Tyson. It would be unfair of me to expect anyone to put up with my drama right now. I want to positively affect someone's life. Not the opposite."

Tyson pulls his hand away from my face, putting it back on the steering wheel. I can still feel the heat on my cheek. He's bothered by my words. I can tell from the look on his face.

"There is going to come a time, Bryce, when I can't wait any longer. There will come a time when I meet someone else, and I know how terrible regrets can be." He looks over at me and then continues through a stop sign. "Look," he says softly. "Nothing is going to change between us, if anything, we are just going to connect on a deeper level."

I feel like he is giving me an award winning sales pitch, but I'm having trouble overcoming my hesitation. *It's not you, it's me.* "You are...nothing short of incredible. I'm definitely not blind or stupid, but I need you to resume your role as my best friend; the reliable, funny, trustworthy guy who doesn't cross boundaries like this." I shift in my seat. "I miss you. I miss us. This pressure is destroying us, and I'm not ready to lose you."

The air grows thick with tension. I glance over at Tyson and he is grinding his jaw, slowly.

Nothing else is said. He pulls up in front of my house, and I pause before exiting the car. "Are we good?"

Tyson continues staring forward, his lips in a tight line. "Yeah," he says in a coarse tone.

I'm still not convinced, so I unbuckle and then lean towards him, pressing my lips to his cheek. Some of the tension alleviates. When I pull away, our mouths are dangerously close. I am breathing his air and he mine. "There aren't enough words in the dictionary to explain how I feel about you. You'll know when I'm ready."

Tyson nods his head gently. "Goodnight."

I reach for the handle, hopping out of his small car. He waves as he drives off. Once in my house, I head straight for my room. My heart is thumping wildly in my chest. I can't stop thinking about Tyson's lips and how close they were to mine. *He's your best friend. You wanted this.* I shake the thoughts off lightly as I undress. My legs are still warm from the alcohol, but that conversation sobered me up.

I catch a glimpse of my imperfect body in the mirror, and I wince. It's been more than a year, and I still want to cry when I see the damage that has been done to it. I find myself disgusting. I pick at my rubbery skin, pulling it from my body to inspect.

No one will ever accept my body the way it is if I can't accept it myself. I'm beyond self-conscious at this point. It's unfair of me to be with anyone until I can learn to love my own body. The silver lining in all of this is that whoever I end up with next will be someone I am madly in love with. It will be someone I trust and feel safe with.

Eight: Making Good on My Assignment

I wake up with a loud groan.

How much did I have to drink last night?

I roll over onto my back, pushing my short hair out of my eyes. The room is spinning and my stomach feels like a tidal wave is rising from the depths. I have a splitting headache and the brightness from the sun sneaking its way through my blinds is paralyzing. I went a bit overboard last night.

When I made it home, I spent the majority of my time puking in the bathroom. No amount of sourdough bread or water could save me.

The worst part of it all? *I remember everything.* The trip to the adult store, the group vibrator choices and purchases, the strip club, and then Tyson.

The bride-to-be was baring it all on stage with the employees of Cheetah's when he rolled up out front. He wanted to take our relationship to the next level, and I was crippled by my fear. My body, our friendship, and my own insecurities all played a role.

I push my short locks off my forehead, staring at the ceiling. *What if Tyson's right? What if I'm not ready for a long time and he meets someone else? What if he really falls for her? What if he gets married?*

I pinch my forehead, my thoughts making the headache worse. *You're doing the right thing.*

I glance at the clock on my nightstand. Ten thirty. Linda has been scheduling appointments more often now that I've been more independent. She knows how significant of a change it has been on my life, and she wants to make sure I can handle it all and I'm not all just talk. She will be here in a little over five hours. I close my eyes and bury my head further into my pillow. I'm hoping that I can sleep this off.

* * *

"A job?" Linda asks, her eyebrows raising, surprised.

I nod, fighting back a smile.

"Bryce, that's fantastic." She is congratulating me, but she is also taking notes on my progress. I wait diligently as she finishes jotting down her thoughts. "First you make it out of the house, and now you're falling right back into normal routines. That is so great. Tell me about it."

"My job?" I ask for clarification.

She nods, her eyes locked on my face.

"I am a receptionist for a local salon, Salon 553."

She continues bobbing her head enthusiastically, taking notes. "How are you liking it?"

I shrug. "I have my first shift tomorrow."

Linda smiles back at me, her light brown eyes gleaming. "That is so exciting."

I nod. It really is. I'm not even sure how it will all go down tomorrow. To say I'm nervous is the understatement of the year.

Linda sets her pen down on her notepad and looks at me. "How are things going with Tyson?"

I sigh. Because Tyson has been my only friend for the past year, he's been a topic of our meetings quite often. Normally I don't mind her bringing him up, as he's always been such a positive influence for me, as far as she's concerned. But now that he's been distancing himself from me, it's different. I'm searching for the right words to explain what is even going on between us when she cocks her head to the side. "Are things alright between the two of you?"

I never mentioned to her about the fact that Tyson tried to kiss me. I guess now is as good a time as any. "When my parents went out of town, Tyson stayed with me so I wouldn't be alone."

She nods. "I remember. That was the weekend you overcame your fear."

I inhale, nodding. "That was also the weekend he tried to kiss me."

Her eyes widen, and then something flashes across her face. I'm curious what she's thinking. She picks up her pen and begins writing. "And how did that make you feel?"

I stifle a laugh. "Um, confused? Pressured? I don't know what I was supposed to be feeling."

She lifts her eyes to mine again. "There is no right or wrong answer, Bryce. The only thing that matters is how *you* felt about it."

I rub my forehead, frustrated. "I was pissed. He made me *feel* upset. We are best friends. We've been best friends since…" I trail off, my voice quivering. "I don't want to lose that."

She nods understandingly. "Were you upset because you don't feel the same way, or were you upset because you're scared to lose that friendship?"

I open my mouth to answer before realizing I'm not even sure *I* know the answer. "I...I..." I swallow, attempting to slow my frantic heart. Suddenly, the beating is pounding loudly inside of my ears, and it's all I can focus on.

Linda looks at me sympathetically. "Bryce, I'm not trying to put you on the spot here. If you're not comfortable answering that, it's okay."

My eyes shift around the room, looking anywhere but into hers. *When did things get so complicated?*

There is an uncomfortable silence before Linda fills it. "Bryce, I'm not going to ask any more questions regarding this issue, but I want you to know that if and when you are ready to talk about it, I will be here."

I nod, still not bothering to look her in the eyes.

She goes back to jotting in her notepad. I glance up at the clock on the wall, thankful that our session is just about up.

"You've made such amazing progress these

past couple of weeks, Bryce. I want you to know how proud I am of you." I glance up, finally finding the courage inside of me to lock eyes with her. Her eyes are non-judgmental and kind.

I force a smile upon my face. "Thank you."

"However, I am worried that you might still be holding yourself back. I'm worried that there may not be enough motivation outside of your new job to keep you moving forward," she says honestly.

I swallow, digesting her words.

"I have a new homework assignment for you," she says, setting her pen down, her brown eyes locking with mine. "I want you to try to make one new friend, either through work or through another avenue."

I nod.

The idea of making a new friend is absolutely terrifying to me, but Linda is right; without Tyson, there isn't much motivation for me out in the real world apart from my job, and it's completely in my power to change that.

* * *

I spend ample time getting ready for my first day of work. I probably change outfits at least six times, looking for something that is business-casual, while also comfortable. I settle on a long sleeve sheer navy blouse and black tank underneath along with black slacks.

Because I'm so anxious, I end up arriving at the salon nearly thirty minutes early. I stay in my car for the next fifteen minutes, attempting to slow my sped up heartbeat. It's not like I've never had a job before. That's not what I'm nervous about. I'm nervous about interacting with all different types of people. Because I've been spending so much time alone, I'm not sure I remember how to play well with others.

I take a deep breath before exiting my car and heading for my new place of employment. As I enter the high-end salon, multiple pairs of eyes stare me down. "Can I help you, dear?" A middle-aged woman with wavy blond hair and a kind smile asks from her station.

I nod. "Actually, it's my first day."

Her eyes trail my body from top to bottom before her smile returns. "Oh my gosh, you must be Bryce!" she exclaims excitedly, stepping away from her client and walking toward me.

Her blue eyes are kind and her smile so big, I'm instantly put at ease. I nod again.

She shuffles over to me, pulling me into a warm hug. "Welcome, welcome, we are so happy to have you."

My eyes shift around to the rest of the hair stylists, which are all focused on our interaction. Some are smiling, some are staring, and at least one is glaring. *Great*. I'm not big on being the center of attention.

"I'm Mel," she says as soon as she releases me from her embrace. She ushers me to the front desk area and motions to it with her hand. "This is going to be your new home. I'll get Janet."

Janet spends the next four hours training me on phone etiquette, the computer system, scheduling appointments, and more and then it's finally time for me to take a lunch break. The salon I work at is unique in the fact that it has a break room for the employees. It's small, only a few round tables and chairs, but there are vending machines, a kitchenette, and even a fridge and microwave. I didn't think to bring a lunch, so I purchase a bag of chips and hope that will suffice until I get off.

There is only one other person in the break

room, so instead of sitting by myself like I normally would, I take Linda's homework to heart and approach a beautiful girl immersed in her phone. "Do you mind if I sit with you?"

She doesn't even bother acknowledging me by looking up, just waves me off. I'm not sure if she is saying it's alright or not okay. I assume the prior and sit down with her anyways. "I'm Bryce," I say, hoping to steal her attention away from her iPhone.

The brunette is tall and leggy, with long straight dark hair and perfect make-up. She finally looks up, gives me the once over, and then her eyes dart back to her phone. "Trista," she says in a bored voice.

She looks like she just walked off the cover of a magazine. She has to be one of the prettiest girls I've ever laid eyes on, but her lack of interest is disheartening.

I open my bag of chips and begin eating them when her eyes shift up to me, and it's as if she's disgusted by my actions. "I'm sorry," I say. "Am I making too much noise?"

She shakes her head and rolls her eyes. She reaches into her black leather purse which is seated next to her on top of the table and pulls out a plastic bag of apple slices. "I can't believe you can eat that crap." She motions with her head toward my bag of chips.

I shrug. "I have a pretty high metabolism. I can basically eat whatever I want as long as I don't go overboard."

She sighs loudly, opening the plastic Ziploc bag in front of her. "Must be nice. I gain weight just by looking at that crap."

My eyes scan her body quickly. I have no idea what she is talking about. She is in better shape than I am. Some might go as far as to say she is overly skinny. "You look great," I say.

Her eyes roam her own body and a disgusted look plays upon her face. "I need to lose five pounds."

I shrug. "I think you're perfect."

She sighs loudly, closing the Ziploc bag and throwing it back in her purse. "I have to get back to work."

She stands up from the table, turning toward the door.

"It was nice to meet you, Trista," I say, watching her go.

She spins around, plastering what I can only assume is a fake smile upon her lips. "You too." And then she exits the break room, leaving me alone.

I'm not sure my assignment is going quite like Linda had hoped, but at least I'm trying.

*   *   *

"You again?" the bartender at Side Bar asks as I sit down at the bar.

I nod. "Me again."

He breaks out into a grin. "What can I get you?"

I stare at the plethora of alcohol situated behind him and decide to make it a simple Jack and Coke.

My first day on the job did not go as smoothly as I would have hoped. The first part of the day was fine, but the last few hours, it seemed like I couldn't do anything right. Not to mention the fact that I was getting the stink eye from Trista. I'm not sure what I did to make her dislike me so much, but if it wasn't obvious that she disliked me before, it's crystal clear now. Especially after she accused me of mixing up her clients appointments and blaming me for being double booked.

The bartender sets the Jack and Coke down right in front of me. "You look like you've had a tough day, so this one is on the house," he says, his eyes warm and welcoming.

I exhale sharply. "Seriously?"

He nods. "You want to talk about it?"

I'm not sure why he is being so nice to me, but it's a welcome change from the complete bitch Trista was to me on my first day. Without much thought, I find myself nodding. "I started my new job today and one of my co-workers was completely rude and unhelpful. I'm pretty sure she hates me, but I don't know why."

He shakes his head like he understands. "Girls can be catty, especially when they are around other attractive females. That's probably all it is. You don't strike me as someone who is malicious."

"I'm not," I reply. I'd forgotten what it felt like to be dogged based off of my looks. It's been so long since I've been around other females. Back in high school, I was popular, but definitely judged. Girls can be nasty.

"Felicia," the bartender calls out to his co-worker. She is the secondary bartender at Side Bar. With pink hair, a nose ring, and tattoos, she's definitely got a punk rock vibe going on for her. She hops over, her eyes shifting between her co-worker and me. "Tell this beautiful lady that she is better than the catty bitches at her work."

Her expression changes to sympathy. "Girl, you are gorgeous. Just remember that you are the bigger person."

I nod, sipping my drink. "Thanks."

"What's your name, darling?" she asks me.

"Bryce."

"Nice to meet you, Bryce." She extends out her hand for me to shake. "I'm Felicia. What are you drinking?"

I look down at my half-empty glass and back up at her. "Jack and Coke."

She shifts her eyes to her co-worker. "Ben, another Jack and Coke on me for this lovely lady."

Ben locks eyes with me. "See? There are some good people out there."

I can't help but smile. Yeah I had a shitty experience with a co-worker…but I've just made two potentially new friends. I'd say today isn't turning out as bad as I had previously thought.

*　　*　　*

I'm feeling good and tipsy as I leave the bar. I'm not drunk by any means, but I am definitely buzzed. Tingles run up the length of my back and neck as I get the intense feeling I'm being watched. It's dark outside, but illuminated by the tall lamp posts lining the small parking lot. I spin around, my eyes darting about, seeking out the culprit. When I see no other people outside, minus a few people on the other side of the street, my speeding heartbeat begins to slow. I'm probably still jittery from my past and everything that has happened with Tyson recently. I climb into my car, locking the door immediately out of habit. *I wish I could have celebrated with my best friend tonight.*

Nine: The Pressure is on

"Salon 553, this is Bryce," I answer the phone. I can see Trista making her way from the parking lot. Her long dark hair is blowing in the wind behind her. She is wearing the smallest pair of white jeans I've seen in a long time and a white crop top. She seems like a girl who can get away with wearing anything at her jobs.

After I schedule the appointment with the customer on the phone and hang up, Trista pulls open the door and walks in.

"Good morning, Trista," I greet her with a warm smile. Her head spins around as she eyes me down and a disgusted look plays upon her face.

She doesn't even bother responding just walks past my area and to her own station. The other hairstylists greet her and get different reactions. I think it's safe to say she still dislikes me for one reason or another.

I have met a couple of really nice hairstylists, who make the job more exciting. They don't get along with Trista, but they really like me.

The rest of the week slides by at a sluggish

pace. My boss is very impressed with me. She tells me I'm catching on quicker than any person who has held the position before me. Trista is still cold and calculating toward me, but I've done my best to avoid her throughout the week.

I'm sweeping the floor when one of the hairstylists approaches me. "My mother-in-law is watching my kids and I really need to get home to relieve her. Are you going to be okay locking up?" Shondra asks.

I glance up at her, my stomach sinking. I was told when hired that I would more than likely be the last person out of the building on most nights, but I guess I just didn't think it would happen this fast. Without much thought, I find myself nodding, plastering a pseudo-smile across my face.

"Great," Shondra says, slipping on her jacket. "You were a big help today, thank you."

"Thanks," I reply, my eyes returning back to the task at hand. My mind is running through everything that is left to be done and how long I will actually be alone. Thankfully, besides sweeping, the only thing I have left to do is empty the trashes and lock up. I hastily finish sweeping and then grab the trash from all the receptacles, bagging it into one larger bag. Our trash bin is located at the back of the building, so I grab my keys to ensure that I don't accidentally get locked out, and make my way outside with the bag heaved over my shoulder. There is a slight breeze, but for it being mid-October, I'm surprised by how unusually warm it is. It's a full moon tonight, and I find myself stopping to stare. It's beautiful in its entirety; big, round, and with a hue of blue. I shake myself out of it after a couple of moments and then begin making my way behind the building to the trash bins. I open the lid and throw the black bag inside and head back inside.

Once I'm back inside the building, I lock the back door, turn off the majority of the lights, and set the alarm after grabbing my personal belongings. Once the alarm is set, I have two minutes to make it out.

As soon as my foot is through the door, I hear the salon phone begin to ring. I know I'm being timed, so my mind goes through a bit of a dilemma. Should I head back inside, kill the alarm and answer it? Or should I leave like I had already been doing? My conscience gets the best of me when I worry that it might be my boss checking up on me. I head back inside, turning off the alarm and catching the phone on one of the last rings. "Hello?"

Silence.

"Hello?" I ask again, to which I don't receive an answer. I swear I can hear someone breathing on the other end, but I chalk it up to a mistake and hang up. I begin to set the alarm once more, when the phone rings yet again.

"Hello?" I answer it without hesitation.

"Bryce, is that you?" A familiar female voice asks from the other end.

"Yes," I reply.

"You're still there?" my boss asks.

"Technically, I was just walking out when you called," I answer. "Sorry I missed your call before, I tried to pick it up in time."

"What call?" Janet asks.

"The one right before this one. When I answered no one was there."

Janet breathes loudly into the phone. "This is the first time I called."

"Oh," I reply, dumbfounded. "Well, I'm just getting ready to head out."

"Okay, good. How did everything go tonight?" she asks.

"Good. I was just cleaning up when Shondra took off."

"Alright. Happy to hear that. Thanks for the great job today!" Janet says enthusiastically.

"You're welcome."

"Have a good night, Bryce," she says.

"You too." I hang up the cordless phone on the base charger once more and set the alarm again. I lock the front door and pull on it to make sure it's secure before heading for my car. It's dark outside, but not pitch dark. When I checked the clock before leaving, it had just passed 9:00 p.m. I breathe in deeply, savoring the feeling. It's been so long since I've felt safe enough to be out in the world late at night, alone. I'm finally gaining my freedom back, and it feels amazing.

*   *   *

I know it's a bad idea before I even get in my car, but that doesn't stop me. I've been trying to get ahold of Tyson this entire week and he's been conveniently checked out. He hasn't been responding to my text messages, my calls, nothing. It's so unlike him, and it has me worried. I don't want to believe that his avoidance is because I shot him down, twice.

Tyson has been there for me more than anyone else in my entire life in the short amount of time we've known each other, I'm not willing to give up our friendship without a fight, much less an explanation. I pull up to the familiar street, and before I even kill the engine, I see an unfamiliar red car parked out in front. I know from experience the car isn't Tyson's or Grae's, but I ignore my nagging suspicion as I park directly behind it. I climb his front porch steps quickly, a bundle of nerves. I'm not sure what I am going to say, how he is going to react, or even if he still wants me in his life. It's killing me inside.

I knock timidly on the front door, and within moments I hear barreling footsteps headed toward me. The door swings open, and I find myself staring at Grae. His facial expression changes from confusion to a bit of shock to pity. "Bryce?" he says and then glances back toward the couch in the living room. My eyes follow his, and sure enough, Tyson is seated on the couch, his back toward me, and his arm around a blond female. Both of their heads swivel in my direction when Grae says my name. *Ashleigh the bimbo.* Tyson's expression mirrors his roommate's.

Grae steps away from the door as Tyson jumps up from the couch startled, and stalks toward me. "Bryce, what are you doing here?"

I can feel the daggers being thrown at me from Ashleigh's eyes. She looks pissed that I am here.

"Can we talk?" I ask, glancing between Tyson, Ashleigh's glare, and Grae's gawking stare. I want to have this conversation in private, not in front of the prying eyes staring us down.

"Um, sure," he says awkwardly, glancing back at Ashleigh, and then stepping out onto the porch and closing the door behind him.

We walk to the edge of the porch and he takes a seat on the ledge, tensely. "What's up?"

My eyes drink him in as I take in his ruffled brown hair and chocolate eyes, realizing this is the first time I've seen him where he hasn't been completely put together, perfectly styled hair and all. I actually prefer it. He is wearing a loose-fitting white t-shirt and light blue jeans. I am beginning to realize just how much I've missed his presence in my life. "You've been avoiding me," I say.

His eyes shift around, dodging mine. "No, I haven't."

"Yes, you have. I must have called you at least ten times and texted double that. I haven't gotten one response back from you."

He rubs his chin, tensely. "I've been busy."

My eyes glance toward the window. "I can see that."

"What do you want, Bryce?" he asks aggressively, in a tone I'm unfamiliar with. He never speaks to me this way.

"What's going on?" I ask, choking up. "Something has obviously changed between us."

His jaw tenses and he looks away. "Bryce, you can't honestly expect me to spend all of my free time with you. I have other friends, a life."

His words cut deeper than anything he's ever said to me before. I feel like I'm looking at a complete stranger, not the person who saved me. I swallow a few times, biting my lip, fighting back tears. "I never once said that, and you know it. You couldn't have sent a simple response back? Do you not consider me a friend anymore?"

He sighs, rubbing his chin. "What do you want from me, Bryce?"

I step back, my balance wobbly. "I want my friend back. I want the person who saved me *that day* back."

He rolls his eyes, sighing. "You're not the same person you were back then, and neither am I." He stands up.

Tears begin spilling over my cheeks, and I keel over, grabbing my stomach. Breathing is becoming a chore, and I'm sucking in air, but it is only making it worse. I'm sobbing and hyperventilating in the worst way. This is the hardest I've ever cried in my life. I feel a pair of arms encircle me and pretty soon, I am pulled tightly into his chest. He is holding me so close, I can smell his cologne mixed with his pheromones, and it is calming me. It takes more than a few minutes for me to quiet my cries and take control of my breathing, but when I do, he finally releases me and takes a step back.

"I feel like everything is changing between us," I whisper through silent tears.

He takes his thumbs and sweeps them under my eyes, wiping the tears away. "Bryce, what did you expect? Guys and girls can't be friends. One or the other will always develop deeper feelings. That's just the way it is."

I shake my head. "No. We were friends…but you had to ruin it."

He steps further away from me. "Bryce, I'm

your friend. I'll always be your friend. But things have changed between us, we both know it. Honestly, I don't think we can go back to the way things were. Not now."

His words feel like a knife twisting inside my gut. "I don't know what I want. I just know that I don't want to lose you."

"Look, I laid my heart out on the line, and you kind of walked all over it. I want you. I've wanted you for a very long time, but I'm not willing to wait forever, Bryce." He sighs, running a hand through his hair. "I have to go back inside. Even if I'm not in your life, I want you to know that I'm always going to be here for you. We've been through too much for me to just walk away now. I just can't continue to hang out with you, and be around you when I know you don't want me the same way as I want you. It's too hard. I won't do it."

I nod, my shoulders slouching, defeated. He slides his fingers beneath my chin, shifting it upwards so he can look me in the eyes. "You're the only person I trust," I say quietly.

He nods. "I know. That's something you're going to have to work on. I believe in you, pretty girl. You just need to have some faith in yourself."

I inhale deeply as he spins around and begins walking toward the door. "Tyson," I call out as he reaches for the handle.

He stops, but does not turn around.

"For what it's worth, you're every girl's fantasy," I say softly.

He pauses for a minute, with his back turned to me. "Not every girl." And then he opens the door and enters his house.

My heart breaks with his last sentence; with the closing of the door. I'm confused, I'm heartbroken, I'm lost. I slowly make my way down the steps of his front porch and back to my car. As soon as I am seated, my head falls against the steering wheel, more tears sliding down my face. I wish things could go back to the way they were before he tried to kiss me, but I know it's not that easy. Everything changed that night. I haven't been with anyone since Robbie, and as much as I want to believe I'm stupid for turning Tyson down and give him everything he wants, the little voice inside of me is too scared. I'm scared that if we go down that road and it doesn't work out, I'll lose him forever. I know I'm going to have to make a choice soon, whether to let him go or pursue the thing that scares me the most. God help me.

Before

* * *

"Hey honey, Tyson is here to see you. Can I send him in?" my mother asks.

I open my eyes weakly, looking back at her. I don't want him to see me like this.

I hear another pair of footsteps coming toward me. I haven't been able to dwell on how bad my body looks because I've been drugged up on pain medication, but I know Tyson is not going to look at me the same way he used to, ever again.

I can barely hold my head up as Tyson takes a couple of hesitant steps toward me. "What did he do to you?" he asks softly.

I am floating between consciousness and in a way, I'm thankful. I won't be able to worry about the way my body looks to him.

"Thank you," I whisper.

Tyson comes in closer, taking a seat in the chair beside my hospital bed and taking my hand in his. "For what?" he asks.

"Thank you for saving me."

He squeezes my hand softly and I sense the sadness radiating off of him. "I wish I would have checked on you sooner. Maybe I could have prevented this."

I shake my head, coughing. "This is not your fault. Robbie found out I was planning to leave him, and he took his revenge. This had nothing to do with you."

Tyson looks wound up and visibly shaken. "He won't get away with this. Karma is a vicious beast. If I ever see his sorry ass again, I'll kill him myself."

"Tyson," I say weakly.

"Oh, I'm sorry, you probably need your rest, don't you?" I nod my head, my eyes already preparing to close. I've had enough of analyzing my crappy existence for one day. I don't know why I survived. I'm angry that I did. Nothing will ever be the same again. No one will ever look at me the same.

I wish I hadn't pulled through.

"You scared the crap out of me," I faintly hear. "How could I have missed it? I could have protected you."

I want to open my eyes so badly, but I have no energy. All the sounds begin to dissipate as I drift off.

Ten: Reverting Back to Past Behaviors

It's been two weeks since I confronted Tyson and he told me he couldn't be around me anymore. Two weeks since we last spoke. It hurts like hell not having him in my life, but I realized he was right. It was unfair of me to ask him to stay in my life after he told me how he truly felt. I can't give him what he so desperately wants, and I would just be holding him back from pursuing other relationships. So I decided to let him go. It hasn't been easy. I still catch myself wanting to text him when I have a bad day, or even a great day. I still find myself dialing his number on impulse.

Honestly, if it wasn't for Ben and Felicia, I don't know that I could have done it; cut off all contact and keep pushing. They've definitely made things a lot easier. I've been drowning my sorrows almost nightly, and they've been there to humor my depression.

It's Halloween, and they both have to work, so they invited me to Side Bar for free drinks and a fun night. Ben said Halloween is one of their busiest nights of the year. Everyone gets dressed up and parties until the wee hours of the morning. Felicia went costume shopping with me a couple of nights ago, and of course tried everything under the sun to get me into a sexy costume, but I prevailed. I haven't told Ben and Felicia what happened to me yet, and I don't want them to look at me any differently, so I've been very careful. Turns out there are not a lot of options when you need your arms and legs to be fully covered, so I ended up choosing a witch costume. Not my ideal choice, but it will work.

The bar is packed when I arrive and my usual parking spot it taken. In fact, the entire parking lot is full. I have to park a block away and walk. Luckily, it's one of the busiest nights of the year, so the streets are filled with people. As I make my way inside, I push past the plethora of people, and see that all the bar stools are filled. There is barely standing room as is. Felicia spots me from the bar and waves enthusiastically. She chose to go with a 50's look. She's wearing a pink poodle skirt which matches her hair pretty nicely, along with a black checkered top and polka dotted hair and neck ties. She is also sporting pink plastic framed cat eye glasses. She looks absolutely adorable. I helped her choose the outfit, and I couldn't be more proud.

She motions with her hand to come up to the bar, so I squeeze through the huge line of patrons still waiting to make their drink orders and lean in so we can hear one another. "Hey lady!" she greets me with a smile. "How do I look?" She grabs the edges of her skirt and spins around for full effect.

"You look great!" I shout over the loud music and overall commotion.

Felicia looks at the guy seated at the bar in front of me. "There's a lady standing behind you that doesn't have a place to sit. Will you be a gentleman and give up your chair?"

He glances back at me with an unhappy look. I'm guessing it wasn't easy getting front row seating tonight. It could also be his terrible choice in costume, which is the cheapest looking Batman get-up I've ever laid eyes on. He turns his head back to her, and Felicia bares her pearly whites at him. "There will be one on the house if you comply."

She seems to be talking his language because he quickly hops off the stool. "Make it a double and you have a deal."

She grins at me. "I can do that."

I trade him spots and sit down on the warm stool. I mouth thanks to her as she prepares his double. My eyes travel to the other end of the bar where Ben is working at top speed to make and deliver drinks. "Oh my God!" I squeal loudly. Ben is wearing a Ring Master costume and his beard has been trimmed so much so that he is now simply sporting a goatee. He looks like a completely different person.

Felicia looks back at me and then her eyes shift to Ben. "I know." She slides a drink to the guy behind me and then begins making another right away. No more than a couple of minutes later, I have a drink in front of me. I stare at it, trying to decipher exactly what it is before smelling it. "Long Island?" I ask.

She nods. "It's Halloween!"

I smile back at her. *It sure is.*

A few hours later, and plenty of drinks in, I'm feeling drunk. My cheeks are flushed, I can't stop giggling, and I'm pretty sure I've gone pee more than fifty times. I've made great friends in the bathroom, and I've been hit on more times than I can count. Some guy in a Freddy Krueger costume keeps buying me drinks from the other end of the bar. I've simply been flashing him my beautiful smile in return, but now that I'm feeling freer than ever and frisky, I decide to take a risk and introduce myself to him. I shimmy over to him, not as gracefully as I'd hoped, and I tap him on the shoulder. He spins around, his piercing grey-blue eyes the only thing I can see with his mask on.

"Hi," I say awkwardly with a wave. "I'm the girl you've been buying drinks for all night." I'm well aware I'm slurring, but I'm feeling good, and my inhibitions are out the window.

He nods, remaining mute.

"I just wanted to come over and introduce myself. My name is Bryce." I shake his hand clumsily, but his grip is firm, tight. Almost as if he doesn't want to let go. "Not much of a talker?" I ask.

Freddy Krueger shrugs, cocking his head to the side.

"Alright, well nice to meet you and thanks for the drinks," I say as I spin around, headed once more for the bathroom. My bladder feels beyond full and that was kind of awkward.

I giggle to myself as I make my way through the crowd. Once I'm finished doing my business, I head for the sink to wash my hands. As I'm staring in the mirror, I realize just how ridiculous I look. My eyes are bloodshot, I have a goofy grin plastered across my face, and my cheeks are pink. I wash my hands thoroughly and then decide to splash a little water on my face. When I look back up at my reflection, I notice someone standing behind me. Freddy Krueger. "This is the ladies' restroom," I say. "Did you accidentally walk in here?"

Slowly, the stranger removes his mask and I go pale white. *Robbie.* I'm screaming bloody murder before I can stop myself. I'm so terrified, I'm frozen in place, simply holding my face, squeezing my eyes closed, and screaming.

He lunges forward, throwing his hand roughly over my mouth and wrapping the other one around my body. He lifts me up, off the ground, and I'm shaking. "You really shouldn't have done that." I can feel his warm breath on my ear and I'm trembling. "See you soon."

He places me back onto the ground, removing his hand from my lips and then slips out the door.

I don't know how long I'm standing there, screaming my lungs out, but I lose time. I feel someone grabbing at me, and I scream even louder. "Bryce! Bryce!" the familiar voice attempts to gain my attention. My eyes fly open, and I'm staring at Felicia. Her eyes are wide and her expression is frightened. "What happened? Are you alright?" she asks worriedly.

I am gasping for breath, gripping onto her for dear life. "*He* was here." I can't even think straight. He found me. *He's going to kill me.*

"Who was here?" she asks, holding me up. "Bryce, I need you to tell me what happened."

I fall to the ground, my knees giving out. Tears begin pouring down my cheeks. "He's going to kill me…he's going to kill me…" I continue to mutter over and over again.

The next half hour goes by in a haze. I'm semi-aware of the fact that they have searched the bathrooms and bar and cannot locate the person in the Freddy Krueger outfit. I'm barely coherent as Ben calls a cab for me, pays for it, and puts me in it. "Bryce, where do you live?" he asks.

I look up at him, confused.

"Bryce, I need to give your address to the cab driver so we can make sure you make it home safely."

I swallow, nodding. "Um, 434 South Main Street," I manage to get out.

He looks up at the driver. "You get that?"

The driver nods.

Ben rubs the side of my arm soothingly. "It's going to be okay. He's going to take you home now. Text Felicia as soon as you make it, alright?" I look up at him and nod in understanding. He closes the door behind me. I look next to me and realize that my purse has made it into the vehicle with me. I feel nauseous like I may puke. I roll down the window of the cab partially, and lean my forehead against the cold glass.

"If you puke, it's double," the cab driver drones from the front.

Everything begins spinning, and I squeeze my eyes shut, breathing deeply. I was really drunk tonight. I haven't drank that much in a very long time. Hallucinations can happen, right? Someone was obviously buying me drinks, but the fact that I saw Robbie in the mirror was clearly my subconscious playing a trick on me. It has to be; except, I can still feel his hand over my mouth, his hot breath in my ear. I'm trembling as I wrap my arms around myself tightly.

If Robbie is still around these parts, he'd never risk giving up his location to reveal himself to me. At least that's what I keep telling myself, but the goosebumps and knot in the pit of my stomach tell me otherwise.

* * *

"Bryce! Bryce! Wake up!" my mother cries, and I feel my shoulders being shaken.

My eyes flutter open, and I'm well aware of the wetness that is filling up at the corners of my eyelids, the warm liquid on my cheeks. My pillow is soaked. *I've been crying.* My eyes meet my mother's chocolate ones, and it's the same look she used to give me back when I first moved home. Sympathy. Her eyebrows are crinkled with worry and she looks exhausted.

"You were having a nightmare," she says softly, stroking my cheek, wiping the tears away.

My hair is sticking to my forehead, and I can feel the sweat pooling inside of my clothes. I sit up, pushing back against my headboard.

"Are you okay?" my mother asks, concerned. You haven't had one of these in a long time.

I nod, breathing deeply. "Yeah, it's probably just a fluke or something."

She sighs. "Alright, then. I'll let you get your rest."

I look at the clock on my nightstand. 3:34 a.m.

My mother exits my room and I'm left in the darkness, alone. I don't know what I saw last night, but I know it felt real. *He* felt real. I pick up my phone, sliding my finger across the screen to unlock it. I find my call log and hover over Tyson's name. As much as I want to talk to him right now, I know it's not fair to either of us. I don't want to use him, and I sure as hell don't want to lead him on. I'm no good for anyone right now. I carry way too much baggage. I can't expect anyone to be okay with dealing with me and all my issues. Tyson deserves better. He deserves to be happy.

* * *

So much for it being a fluke. The nightmares have only gotten worse. I've started sleeping with my closet light on. Because my sleep patterns have been so terrible, and I've been overly anxious, I've called into work the past couple of days. Janet warns me that if I can't make it in before the end of the week that she is going to have to find someone to replace me. Today is Friday, and I have no intention of leaving my safe haven. I haven't left my room for anything other than using the restroom and refilling my water. It's too difficult for me to see the looks on my family's faces. I can see the disappointment from a mile away. Mikey isn't even speaking to me. I wish I wasn't such a fuck-up. The only thing I can find motivation to do lately is to sleep. I've been sleeping all day and staying awake all night. I find that my nightmares are not as frequent or as terrifying that way.

I hear the doorbell ring and I make my way over to my window. Linda's car is in the driveway. *This can't be good.*

"Bryce!" I hear my mother call from downstairs.

I glance at my reflection in the mirror. My short brown hair is greasy and flat, my eyes are dull and lifeless, and the pajamas I wear are the same ones I've been wearing all week. I can't recall the last time I brushed my teeth. I'm not sure anyone is prepared to handle me in my current state.

"Bryce!" my mother calls out again.

I open my door and peek my head out. "What?"

"Linda is here to see you," she calls up the stairway.

I close my eyes, inhaling deeply. "Our appointment isn't until Wednesday," I reply.

My mother ascends the stairs halfway so she

can make eye contact with me. "Bryce, we're worried about you, so I called her. Please make yourself presentable and come down."

I groan, closing my door. I guess I won't be able to avoid this confrontation. Quickly, I throw on a pair of sweats and a long-sleeve t-shirt. I brush my teeth until my tongue can't feel anymore grime on them and then I toss a handful of baby powder in my hair, running my fingers through it to make sure the white powder isn't visible before I head downstairs.

Linda is waiting in our usual meeting place when I enter the room. Her green eyes fixate on me as I walk to my normal chair and plop down into it. "Hey, Bryce," she greets me softly.

I glance at her, acknowledging her with a small nod. She grips her notepad close, leaning in. "How are you doing?"

"I'm fine," I reply, instinctually.

Her expression softens. "How about the truth?"

I sigh, shifting uncomfortably in my seat. "I lost my job."

She nods, writing. "I heard. Want to tell me

what happened?"

Not really. I really just want to pretend like this is all a bad dream. In one moment I went from having everything I ever wanted back again to the scared, terrified girl I was last year. I took one step forward and three steps back. "I've been having trouble sleeping lately."

"Nightmares?" Linda asks.

I nod, shying away from her stare.

"I thought we were past those?" she questions, jotting down notes.

I sigh. "So did I."

"What happened, Bryce? You were making such great progress. Your mother was telling me how amazing you were doing at the salon. What changed?" Linda presses me.

I saw Robbie. Only, I'm not sure if it was real or a hallucination. I know how crazy I sound, and I can remember the way Ben and Felicia stared at me that night. I don't know if I can handle anyone else looking at me the same way. I used to tell Linda everything. She was my equivalent to a friend. Someone I trusted. But I know how disappointed she is already in me. If I tell her I saw Robbie at Side Bar on Halloween, she may want to have me committed. It doesn't make sense that he would still be in town, after everything. The police have been looking for him for over a year, following dead lead after dead lead. If he was smart, he would be half way across the country, not in the same city he committed the crime.

I shrug, remaining silent, lost in my thoughts.

Linda continues writing, her shoulders slouching in defeat. After an eternity of silence, Linda decides I'm a lost cause and packs up to leave. I stay rooted in place.

"Well?" I hear my mother ask beneath the closed door.

"Something happened, and she's reverting back to her old ways," Linda replies. "I fear it is only going to get worse."

"Well, what do you recommend?" my mother asks in a worried tone.

"I think I need more sessions with her. I think we need to double them up."

Right after my attack, I used to see Linda three times a week. And then, once she felt like I was making progress, she reduced the sessions to once a week. I feel hopeless. I've worked so hard to gain my freedom back, and he has once again stolen it from me. I fear that I'm never going to be able to escape the hell he's put me in. I fear that I will never be fully healed.

Eleven: Hidden Feelings Surface

"Bryce, I'm worried about you," Linda says, setting her pen down on her notepad. "Your mother says you haven't left your room in over a month. She says you're barely eating and judging by the way your clothes are fitting, I'm going to take her word for it. You don't look healthy."

I pick at my fingernails, keeping my eyes averted from her judging gaze.

"I don't even know if me being here is helping anymore." She sighs. My eyes fall on her. She looks defeated, at her wits end. "You haven't spoken to me in weeks. I think this may be our last meeting together.

No! my mind screams. Although I've been depressed and distracted, Linda has been my only form of human contact besides my family. I don't want to lose her. I want to tell her I'll be better. I want to convince her to stay…but I can barely find the motivation to get out of bed most days. I have no energy and sometimes, I think everyone would be better if I wasn't around.

Linda stands, packing her notepad and pen into

her briefcase. "Bryce, I want you to know that I am always here for you. Just because I won't be coming around any longer, does not mean that you can't reach out to me, day or night, whenever you feel ready to talk again." She walks over to me, gripping my shoulder and squeezing it lightly with her hand. "Take care, Bryce."

I watch her walk out, remaining mute. She opens the front door wide, looks back at me one last time, and then exits. I sigh deeply as I watch her go. *Why can't I just be normal?*

My mother peeks her head in, grinning at me. I can tell she is holding back. She has been ever since I stopped coming out of my room. I wonder if she thinks I'm a lost cause. "How did it go today?" she asks.

My eyes lock with hers as I stand. "Linda quit today."

"She what?" my mother cries.

I shrug. "She quit. She doesn't think there is anything she can do for me."

My mother's eyes widen. "Can she do that?"

I nod. "I think she just did."

My mother steps further into the room, her brown eyes trained on me. "Honey, you need to talk to someone; to me, your father, or even Tyson."

My heart clenches when she says his name. I break her stare and look away sadly. "Tyson doesn't want to be friends anymore."

My mother's face wrinkles with confusion. "What? No, that doesn't sound like Tyson."

I stifle a sob. "Oh, but it is." I brush past her out to the hallway, and then race up the stairs to my room. I close the door behind me, pushing my back up against it, and sliding to the floor slowly. I can see it in all of their eyes—judgement. I know they think I'm a nuisance, a letdown.

* * *

2 Weeks Later

Knock, knock.

Knock, knock.

I'm not deaf. I can hear the knocking, but I'm too tired. Maybe if I just close my eyes again, they will give up.

"Bryce?" I hear the door creek open and the familiar voice ask.

Shit. I grab the comforter closely and pull it up over my head, sliding down underneath it.

I hear footsteps and then feel someone putting their weight on my bed by sitting down on it. I grip the comforter tighter over my face.

"Bryce," he says again softly, but this time I feel a hand rubbing over my body atop the blanket. My whole body tenses when I feel his touch.

He sighs and then removes his hand.

"Look, your mom asked me to stop by. I know we haven't talked in a while, but she is worried about you." I'm dying to see what he looks like. It's been a little more than a month, but most days I feel like I am losing parts of him; forgetting him. I roll over so that my back is facing him.

He shifts on the bed. "What happened?" he asks so quietly I have to strain to hear it. I swallow, my heartbeat speeding up. "Why won't you talk to me?" I can hear how hurt he is by his tone.

I can't bear to see the disappointment in his

eyes. I've been dealing with my mother and father's already...I can't bear to let him down. They all deserve better than me. Someone who can function normally. Someone who doesn't live their life in constant fear. It would be better if I wasn't holding them all back.

"I can't help you if you won't talk to me," Tyson warns. After several moments of complete silence I hear him sigh loudly, the extra weight on my bed being lifted. "You're better than this. The Bryce I know may not be the strongest, but she never gives up. You're giving up."

My heartbeat continues to thump deeply in my chest.

I hear my door close moments later. *He left.* I throw my cover off quickly, running to the window just as Tyson opens our front door. He walks out with his head held low, looking defeated. I wanted nothing more than to talk to him, but after our conversation the last time we spoke, it didn't feel right. He is trying to move on with his life, past me, and if he gets tangled in my drama, that will never happen. I feel disappointed and lost. Tyson still must care about me because he bothered to come out at all. What if I was wrong to push him away? What if I've been a coward this entire time?

* * *

I'm awoken by frantic knocking on my door. I open one of my eyes slightly, glancing at my bedside clock. My eye fights to adjust to the darkness when my mind registers the bright numbers. 2:45 a.m. My heart begins pounding roughly. I throw my comforter and sheet off of my body and rush to the door, opening it. My mother is standing on the other side, her long wavy brown hair disheveled with bloodshot eyes. She doesn't have to bother saying a word, her facial expression says it all. Something is desperately wrong. My stomach plummets and I can feel the knots forming inside.

"Tyson," my mother gasps.

The moment his name leaves her lips, I'm fully awake. "What about Tyson? Is he okay?" There is apparent worry and fear in my voice.

Her face is fallen, appearing sympathetic.

"St. Joseph's," my mother says the familiar hospital name.

I feel like I've just been shot up with adrenaline. I am running around my room like a chicken with its head cut off, throwing on new clothes and shoes, and then grabbing my cell phone and purse. I can't think about the fact that I am leaving the house for the first time in a month. The only thing I can focus on is my best friend's condition. My mother didn't give me any details, just the tip that he is in the hospital.

When I arrive at the hospital, I am led into the waiting room where Tyson's friends and family are congregated. I recognize Tyson's mother instantly. I've seen a couple of pictures of her through Tyson, but her facial structure and her long wavy hair make her look like his older sister.

"Joanne?" I ask, reaching my hand out to grab her shoulder gently.

She spins around, her eyes trailing me from top to bottom. Her eyes are red and puffy, a combination of no sleep and crying, I'd wager. Confusion spills across her face, and she tries to connect the dots.

"I'm Bryce," I offer with a hesitant smile.

"Bryce," she says with a long exhale of air. "I've heard so much about you. Tyson really thinks highly of you." She wraps her arms around me tightly, pulling me into a hug. It's a little close for comfort, but it's nice.

"What happened?" I ask, my eyes darting

throughout the full waiting room. *I wonder if anyone has seen him.*

"He was at home. Someone rang the doorbell. When he opened the door, they opened fire," his mother says, her eyes glistening. "His own house."

My heart begins pulsating quickly as I think of how unsuspecting Tyson would have been, and how terrified he would have felt after being struck by the bullets. "Who would want to hurt Tyson?" I ask incredulously.

She shrugs, sighing. "This person knew exactly where he lived and didn't hold back. They intended to kill him. This was pre-meditated and malicious."

I nod stiffly. "How bad is it?"

"He's in surgery now. He lost a lot of blood." Her facial expression is full of sorrow. I'm sick to my stomach with worry. *He better pull through this.*

*   *   *

I've been sitting here for hours. I can barely keep my eyes open, but I'm terrified that if I give in, I'll miss an important update. My conscience won't allow me such a luxury as sleep. My eyes widen as I see an important looking hospital employee come out in blue scrubs. He is middle-eastern, probably in his forties, and looks just as exhausted as the rest of us. Everyone's eyes and ears perk up as he approaches Tyson's mother and father. I stand up, inching toward the group now surrounding him.

"Tyson made it out of surgery. He is stable. He had a collapsed lung, lost a lot of blood, and has a few blood clots, but his recovery is promising," the doctor tells us.

Tyson is okay. Thank God he's okay…

"When can we see him?" his mother asks.

"He is on a lot of pain medication right now and could use his rest. I'd say give him a couple of days to come around."

I don't need to be told any more. I feel confident enough now to go home, clean myself up, get some rest, and come back in a day or two. After saying my goodbyes, I make my way out to the parking garage and head back home.

All I can think about is our last conversation on his porch and how badly it hurt when Tyson said he couldn't be around me anymore. I'm starting to question my feelings now. I'm beginning to confront my fears.

I take a seat inside my car and let my thoughts take over.

Have I been stupid for turning Tyson down? Have I been a coward? I can't deny that he makes my life better. He is the light in my darkest of days. I'm terrified to lose him. He makes me a better person.

I love him.

I gasp, throwing a hand over my mouth in complete and utter shock.

So, that just happened...

Twelve: Caught

I expected to have a run-in with my parents when I got home, as it is well past their working hours. What I did not expect to see was my therapist, standing beside them. I can smell an intervention from miles away. I'm enraged. *This is what is important to them right now?* While Tyson is laying in a hospital bed, fighting for his life? My mother has an awkward smile plastered on, and I can read her guilt. My father remains stiff and rigid, unwavering. And then there's Linda. She looks conflicted.

"Is this really happening right now?" I ask, bitterly. I can expect this from my father, but my mother? I feel betrayed.

"Bryce, we are here to help you," my mother says softly.

I chuckle. "*Right*," I reply, sarcasm dripping from my voice.

"Come on in, Bryce," Linda says from the couch.

I walk slowly into the living room, the heat from the eyeballs on me, scorching. "Please, take a seat," Linda instructs me.

"No, I think I'd rather stand," I say, crossing my arms across my chest.

Linda nods. "That's alright too."

"You do know that Tyson is in the hospital right now, correct? And that I've been there for the past eight hours? I just want to sleep and then go back." I pause for a second, and then realize I'm not finished. "Look, I know exactly what this is, and I appreciate it, but I'm fine."

My mother's face falls. "Bryce, you haven't been fine in a very long time. We just want to help you get back to normal."

I glare back at her; a mix of emotions are rising up from the depths. I'm angry, I'm hurt, but worst of all, I miss him. Talk about Stockholm syndrome. I feel dirty; I feel cheated.

"My boyfriend who I thought loved me, knocked me out, poured gasoline on me, and set me on fire because he found out that I wanted to leave him. The police never found him, and I've never felt safe. I'm sorry I've been having trouble adjusting to life after that. I didn't know there was a specific healing period." I can't help the tone of my voice, it's hurt and quivering. "He tried to kill me. I'll never be the same person ever again."

Their faces hold matching expressions: pity. "Just let me get some rest so I can go back to see Tyson, and then I will find somewhere new to live."

My mother jumps to her feet. "Bryce, we never said you can't live here."

I glower back at her. "No, you didn't, but I think it's time I move out. I've been a nuisance far too long."

My father stands, puffing out his chest. "Now Bryce, don't be silly."

I stare him down, my eyes cold and firm. "It's time for me to grow up. Throw me in the deep end, see how long I can keep my head above water."

Linda doesn't dare interrupt our squabble, instead she just sits back and watches it all go down.

"Fine," my father says, although glaringly unhappy. "Go on."

I don't waste another second, instead just run up the stairs and to my room. I know I am overreacting, but it's not the time nor place to be focused on my issues. Tyson is fighting for his life. That is what is important. It's been all about me for the past year. It's time to shift the focus.

* * *

There are tubes connected to multiple areas on his body. He looks weak and vulnerable. I've never seen Tyson like this before. I can barely handle it. Every time I stare, I want to vomit. I'm wrecked. I approach his bedside slowly, tip-toeing. I don't want to disturb him at all.

His eyes open and they lock on me, electricity tingles up my back. He looks medicated and tired, yet surprised. I'm nervous to touch him in fear I will hurt him, but I can't help the urge to hug him. I press my head up against his gently. "I don't know what I would have done if you were…" I trail off, sucking in a shaky intake of air. I shake my head lightly. "I'm so sorry for everything. I'm so sorry I pushed you away. I was scared."

His eyes widen as they roll upwards and then closed. I watch him intently, worried, and then he opens his eyes slowly, a tear slipping down the side of his face. It tears me up to see him upset. I stop the tear in its track with my lips. I feel a volt of electricity zap through my body. "I don't mean to upset you," I whisper, leaning my forehead against his. "That's the last thing I want.

I feel a hand grip my arm lightly and I realize he has reached out for me. The way he is looking at me tells me that I'm forgiven. "What happened?" I ask.

He shakes his head dismissively pulling his hand back. "I don't know," he says through labored breaths. "It all happened so fast. All I can even remember is opening the door. I can't even remember what the shooter looked like."

"Do they know who did it?" I probe further.

He shakes his head again. "When I gave my statement this morning, the police mentioned that they were still working on leads."

I feel like I've been as strong as I can be for one day. I know the doctor urged that we stay calm so as to not upset Tyson, but my emotions are boiling over. Tears are burning the backs of my eyes before I can utter another word. I throw my hand over my nose and mouth in an attempt to stifle my cries. I go as far as turning around so my back is to Tyson.

"Bryce," he says in a pained voice. "What's wrong?"

I spin back around, my eyes glossy. "I was so scared I was going to lose you."

He reaches out for me. "But you didn't. I'm alive, and I will heal."

I release a breath of relief. "Do you have any idea how much you mean to me?"

He brings my hand to his lips and kisses it. "Bryce, we don't have to do this now."

"No, you don't understand. I want to talk about this," I say. He continues to hold my hand, but I can tell I have his full attention. "I'm sorry I've been so stubborn and stupid," I begin. "I was blind. I didn't realize what was right in front of me. What's always been right in front of me." I inhale deeply, feeling the effects of my words reverberating through my chest. "You've always been my savior. I was afraid of losing our friendship, so I kept pushing my feelings for you away, but I would rather try to have a relationship with you than live a life full of regrets and what if's. Tyson, I love you."

He inhales deeply, his facial expression full of passion. He doesn't bother responding verbally, instead pulls me into him until our lips meet. I try to stay gentle and not put any pressure on him, but it's difficult with how deeply he is kissing me. It leaves me breathless. Like I need my oxygen fix and he's got it. *I don't know why I didn't try this before…*

We spend the next hour wrapped up in each other when his mother finally comes in and asks for some alone time with her son. I oblige, but offer to make a pit stop at Tyson's house to pick him up his iPod and a change of clothes. I have every intention on coming back to the hospital. After all, I'm not sure I have a home to return to.

*   *   *

When I pull up to Tyson's house, the street lamps illuminate the curb where I park beside, and I make my way up his porch. The motion sensor light shines on me as I make it to the front door. The house is dark inside, and after a few quick peeks through the window, I make the assessment that Grae is not home.

Luckily, I thought this far ahead, because I asked Tyson where the spare key might be hidden in case Grae was MIA upon my arrival. I find the spare key under a dead pot of flowers, and let myself inside without issue. I hit the switches as I pass by rooms, lighting up the darkened spaces. Tyson's room is upstairs, so I scurry up the stairs and into the bedroom I know to be his. Clothes are strewn about all over the bed and floor and the OCD part of me can't move on until I clean up the mess. Without knowing whether they are clean or dirty, I end up chucking the whole pile into his dirty clothes hamper. I spot his iPod sitting on his desk, connected to the computer via a USB cord. I unplug it and throw it inside my purse. My eyes scan the room, landing on the closet. I hurriedly rush over and end up finding a pair of light grey sweatpants, a white crew neck t-shirt, socks, and a pair of boxer-briefs.

As I'm about to leave his room and make my descent back downstairs, I hear the front door close. *Grae must have gotten home.* I scoop the clothes up in my arms and begin making my way down the stairs. I'm expecting to come face to face with Tyson's roommate, but he isn't in the living room. I double back toward the stairs and peek my head into the room I know to be his. It's darkened and no one answers when I call out his name.

I could have sworn I heard the front door close. I take hesitant steps toward the front door, noticing the motion sensor flood light is still on. After peeking out the window, I open the door and stick my head out. The driveway is empty and my car is the only one out in front of the house. The air is cooler now, and I shudder as I close the door, bumps rising all over my arms and legs.

I need to go turn off the lights I've switched on since I arrived. I spin around, headed in the opposite direction, when I run into a stiff object. I swivel my head up and I lose control of my bladder. The warm liquid is trailing down my legs. *Robbie.*

I drop the clothes I am holding and twirl around, instantly grabbing for the handle when I feel the impact of something hard and cold against my skull and I go flying toward the ground. My eyes are closed before I crash to the floor roughly.

Before

* * *

"Oh, I'm so sorry." I pull my hand back quickly.

The person whose hand I just grazed turns his eyes to me. They are intense and beautiful, making my heart race. "I'm sorry." He chuckles, casting his eyes downward. "Go ahead." He motions with his head toward the book I had previously been grabbing.

I reach up on my tip-toes once more, grabbing the infamous book from the top shelf. "Was this the book you were reaching for too?" I ask, holding the book on the Revolutionary War out for him to see.

He nods, smiling. "My teacher uses it in our American History class."

"Oh, yeah?" I ask. "Where do you go to school?"

"ASU," he replies, shifting the weight of his backpack around.

"Me too." My eyes light up. "Who's your teacher?"

"Mr. Bonham," he says, pausing to see if it registers.

I shrug. "I have Mrs. Jefferson."

He nods. "I'm Robbie." He reaches out a hand, taking mine delicately into his own and shaking it.

"Bryce," I say, fixated on his handsome outward appearance.

"Well, it looks like there is only one copy. Would you be opposed to sharing it with me, Bryce?" Robbie asks. I shake my head no, semi-out of it. He is charming, handsome, and mysterious.

Please tell me you're my next mistake.

I lead the way to a back table where we can share the book. There is absolutely no way in hell he's not checking out my ass as we walk. I make sure to shimmy back and forth seductively as he follows. I plan to have him eating out of the palm of my hand in a few hours.

Thirteen: Praying for a Miracle

I come to in an unfamiliar room. It's cold in here, and everything looks older and concrete. There aren't any windows in the room, and it's barely furnished, minus the small twin size bed, dresser, and two person table. My eyes continue scanning the small area, and I'm starting to believe that I'm in a basement somewhere.

I look down at my clothes and realize that I have been changed. I am now in grey sweats which are a few sizes too big for me and a white t-shirt. He cleaned me up. *He saw everything.* My cheeks hurt like hell from the duct tape across my lips. My hands and feet are duct taped to a chair. There is something weird going on with my forehead, like something is sticking to it. My eyes fall on Robbie and I know now he isn't some figment of my imagination. Besides his unruly facial hair and overgrown mane, Robbie looks about the same as he always has. His eyes stay constant with their chilling blue irises. My heart begins beating erratically, my eyes shifting frantically around the room, looking for anything to fight back with; looking for a way out.

"Well, well, look who's finally awake," Robbie taunts me as he inches closer. I lean as far back in my chair as I can. I don't want that monster anywhere near me. His facial expression softens as he approaches. "God, you're so beautiful. You've always been so God damn beautiful. But you knew that already…didn't you?" He sits down on the edge of the bed, pulling my chair so that I am facing him. "I changed your clothes. I behaved, scouts honor." He salutes me. "I just knew how embarrassed you would be if you woke up and realized you pissed your pants."

I had peed the bed a couple of times when we were together. It was always when I was in the middle of a nightmare. Robbie used to belittle me. He used to rub my nose in it like I was some kind of fucking animal. He always said, "You want to be treated like an adult? Then act like one."

I squint back at him, wondering what I ever saw in the loser.

He slams his palm to his forehead. "Why did you have to ruin everything? I loved you so God damned much!"

I can't answer, even if I want to.

I feel his hands grip my legs right above my knees, and I shudder beneath his touch. He doesn't even notice my reaction. "It's really a shame too. You were a perfect canvas until the accident."

I want to break free and lunge at him; wrap my delicate fingers around his thick neck and choke the life out of him. I've never loathed someone as deeply as I do my ex-boyfriend. Not to mention the fact that I am still as terrified to death of him today as I was a year ago. I may be even more timid because of everything that has transpired since that day.

Robbie grins back at me, sadistically. "Do you recognize where we are?" he asks animatedly, standing up and spinning around.

My eyes follow him, but nothing comes to mind.

He gives me a disappointed look and then sighs. "I'm hurt." He throws his hand over his chest dramatically. "But I guess I'll tell you." He strides over to the table and picks up a framed photo, holding it up in front of my face.

It is a picture of Robbie and me from when we first moved into our new house, next door to Tyson. It was six months before he lit me on fire. I remember how disillusioned I was. I remember my goofy grin standing in front of something that we shared. I was so proud. He pulls the picture back and stares at the glass lovingly. He strokes the picture a few times with his fingers before setting it back down on the table. "Remember that day?" he asks. "You were making me take a million pictures because we finally got our own place. That place was the beginning of us and also the untimely end. That place is our relationship. This was always *our place.*" The way he emphasizes his last words make me think he is giving me a hint of some kind. My eyes scan the concrete walls and ceiling before they land back onto Robbie's grinning face. *It can't be.*

"You know I cleared out of here for a couple of weeks after everything went down. The police were looking for me everywhere and I managed to lie low, but after a while people started to forget. So I returned, but they were already clearing our stuff out of the house, so I found a loophole. I remembered the time I used to spend in the basement, and I can still remember when we used to play hide and seek, and your favorite hideout."

I swallow digesting his words. My eyes continue to travel along the walls and I realize that the reason I didn't recognize the room is because it's furnished. Before when we lived in the house this room was hidden and bare.

"So I found a bed and some other furniture and I was set up in my new room before they ever rented it out again. It was the perfect set up."

My stomach drops as I realize that Robbie never actually left, it was merely an illusion I convinced myself to believe in; a healing tactic. He's known my every move. He's been following me longer than back on Halloween. Chills run throughout my body.

I remember how deeply I fell for him after I first met him and how quickly. There were signs from the beginning I chose to ignore: his short temper, the unwarranted jealousy, and his low blows during arguments. It wasn't until we moved in together that things began to escalate to the next level. I still remember the way it felt after he laid his hands on me the first time, how stunned I was.

"You know, I never wanted any of this. All I ever wanted was you. I thought I wouldn't ever see you again after everything, but it's like I'm getting a second chance, and I want to do it right this time. Now that we're finally back together, I am going to prove my love to you."

I'm having trouble breathing because of the duct tape on my lips and because I'm scared to know what he means by proving his love to me. He reaches his hand out to touch my chin and my whole body convulses, and I begin sobbing.

"I've been following you for a while, Bryce. I was there the day you took your first steps out of the house, the day you landed your new job. I was there on Halloween, and I gunned Tyson down in his own home." He stops, beaming. "He didn't even see it coming. The difficult part was getting the gun. Would you believe I stole this off a police officer?"

I'm trembling with fear and choking on my tears.

"I'm going to remove the tape across your mouth, but you have to promise not to scream."

I shake my head in a yes fashion enthusiastically knowing the minute he frees my mouth I am screaming for help.

As soon as I feel the cool air meet my lips, I'm screaming as loud as humanly possible. "Help! Help me!" I see his hand coming at my face before my mind registers the pain to follow. He backhands me so hard, the chair I am strapped to falls to the ground with a loud thud. My cheek is on fire and throbbing from the impact, even my shoulder feels injured from the fall.

"Shhh." He motions with a finger over his lips when there are audible footsteps coming from above us. I see Robbie's feet approaching and then I am pulled back into a seated position.

"Why are you doing this?" I ask, my lip quivering in fear.

"Because dear, I love you so God damn much, and I can't bear to see you with anyone else. We are soulmates. You're mine and you've always been," he says in a controlling tone. "Why do you think I cut Tyson's brakes and then shot him? He's just an obstacle for us. He always has been."

The beating of my heart intensifies as he continues to brag about the fact that Tyson is in the hospital. *I should have known.*

The only thing that I can focus on right now is staying alive. The only way that can happen is if I free myself from my restraints. "I have to go to the bathroom," I try another tactic entirely.

"No worries, babe." Robbie slips out of the room so quickly, I almost miss him. He returns seconds later with a white plastic bucket. It looks like the same type of one my mother uses for mopping. He places it in front of me and I stare from the duct tape holding me in place to the bucket and back again. *There is no way he expects me to pee in that.* He motions with his head toward the bucket. "I can't trust you to go to the bathroom without raising hell so this is your only option."

I glance back at my restraints, swallowing. "No thanks, I'll just hold it."

He cocks his head to the side. "Suit yourself." He places the bucket back down on the hard floor.

"So, you have me, what now?" I ask in an attempt to pull more information out of him in regard to what he plans to do to me.

Chandelier by Sia begins playing inside my pocket and my eyes follow Robbie's frantic ones. My speakers are pretty dominant, even with the phone cloaked inside of my pocket, and I can see the anger flashing across his face. His eyes shoot up toward the ceiling when we hear audible footsteps headed toward the basement door. There is a creak, and we can now clearly hear someone making their way down the stairs. Robbie races around to me and places the tape back across my lips. He grabs the phone out of my pocket and chucks it at the ground. I can tell without even looking that he has shattered the screen. The sound of the impact is piercing. He turns his back to me, and begins to make his way toward his obstacle. I try to scream with everything in me, but the tape is so tight across my mouth, I'm just running out of breath. The tape is even more restricting this time around. It muffles my scream, but Robbie whips his head back around after a few moments and throws a punch right at my stomach. I feel like all of the air has been knocked out of me, and I am gasping for a deep breath; a difficult thing to do when your mouth is blocked.

I lift my head just in time to see Robbie grabbing his gun and cocking it. I'm shaking from fear.

"Hello?" A male voice calls out from the other side of the thin wall. And then we hear the dresser that cloaks the door being slid across the floor. My eyes are wide as Robbie shoots a quick glance my way and then back to the door, lifting the gun.

I see the door handle slowly turning and I'm accidentally holding my breath, forgetting my circumstances. I see a handsome Hispanic male in his early twenties peek his head around the door. His eyes widen in fear as Robbie steps closer to him, the gun aimed at his head. "If you say another word, you're dead," Robbie warns.

Robbie reaches out and pulls the terrified man into the room. "Get down on your knees," he orders in a sharp tone.

The poor guy looks terrified. I'm terrified for him. He shifts his eyes nervously from Robbie to me and then back toward the door. *He's going to flee.*

Don't leave me here! Don't leave me with him! Seconds later he is making a run for it. Robbie pulls the trigger before he even makes it past the threshold. The injured stranger lets out a grunt and then falls face forward onto the hard floor.

There are frenzied footsteps above us and now I can hear a female voice shouting. The door opens with a creak and I hear the sound of heels clacking against the wooden steps. Robbie looks at me with a devilish grin and then he slinks backward into the room so she doesn't see him right away.

"Oh my God! Oh my God!" she screams loudly. "No! No! No!" she continues repeating, unstable.

Robbie quietly approaches the doorframe, but the blond is too focused on the dead male to notice. Her shoulders are heaving up and down as she presses her ear to his chest and her arms wrap tightly around his cold body.

"Why today?" Robbie asks, capturing the female's attention immediately.

She screams so shrilly I have chills running down my spine. She stumbles backward from the door and then spins around taking off in a full run toward the wooden staircase. She's out of my eyesight when I hear the deafening sound of the gun going off again, and the chilling sound of her body falling to the ground roughly. I wince, squeezing my eyes closed. *I'm going to die today.*

Right after I was lit on fire, there were times when I didn't know if I wanted to go on. Being dead meant life would be easier for me, but it was only because I didn't know my full potential. Now that I've been able to experience what life is supposed to be, I want to savor it. I want know what it feels like to grow old. I want to know what it feels like to have a family. I'm tired of taking the easy way out. I'm ready to take my life back.

Of course I would realize this during my last moments. I haven't believed in God in a really long time, but given the circumstances, I'm willing to change my opinion. I press my hands together, which are bound, ignoring the foreign feeling and close my eyes, letting the words spill out of me.

Fourteen: Justice is Served

It's been hours since Robbie shot two people in the basement of our old house. He hasn't been back to the room I'm in since. The only thing that did happen was he pulled the body of the male out of the doorway so I wasn't simply sitting there staring at it. I've heard terrifying noises such as chopping, a chainsaw, and now eerie silence, and a strong smell of bleach. The sound of crinkling plastic makes my stomach churn. My imagination is running wild with frightening visions of what he's done to those poor people.

I scoot my chair quietly across the floor stopping abruptly when it makes a rubbing sound. My heart is pounding against my chest as my eyes stay trained on the open door. I breathe out a sigh of relief when I hear the chainsaw start up again. I scoot once more stopping directly in front of a table where a knife is sitting near the edge. Maneuvering my hands down while they are still tied behind my back is a sight to see, but the minute I feel the blade touch my fingers, I know it's all worth it.

My hands are tied so tightly behind my back there is no possibility of me being able to cut the duct tape without immediately dropping the knife. The only thing I can really do with 100% certainty is to grip it like my life depends on it.

My thoughts shift to my family…how they are going to react when he cuts me up into tiny pieces and ships me to them one by one? My imagination is obviously running wild, but I can't help it. The mixture of stenches coming from the other room is making me nauseous. *If I ever get out of here, I am going to tell my brother I love him.* He's annoying, that's just what brothers are, but I do love him. I remember the first time I ever held him in my arms. I remember how tiny he was and how scared I was that I might drop him.

"What should we name him?" my mother asks weakly from the hospital bed.

I glance back at the tiny creature in my arms. His ears are big and round and a name instantly pops into my head. "What about Mikey?" I offer up. He reminds me of Mickey Mouse, but this way he won't be bullied over his name.

My father chuckles. "I like that."

I nod, my eyes fixated on my baby brother.

"I think it's perfect," he says, walking over and kissing me on the top of the head.

Hours later, after losing myself in a series of memories, Robbie pokes his head in with a disturbing smile. "Gosh, you have no idea how good it feels to finally have our house back."

I think I'm going to be sick. He killed two innocent people without a second thought or any remorse. There's nothing to say that he won't do the same to me. He reaches his hand out to the back of my neck and slips it around, chills immediately following. Robbie stares down at me beneath furrowed brows and then darts his eyes around the room nervously. "Where is it?"

I swallow knowing that I've been found out. *He's going to kill me with the weapon I'm using to protect myself, how ironic is that?* I keep a stone face as he backhands me brutally and my head whips backward. I feel a pop beneath my skin and then blackness begins seeping in obscuring my sight.

* * *

I come to, the pain in my face intense, I feel like someone is stabbing me in the face repeatedly every time I blink. Unfortunately for me, that's every few seconds. My eyes stroll around the room, taking in the familiar wallpaper and trim. *I never thought I'd be in this room ever again.*

My wrists are aching from the ties around them. I'm tied to bed posts this time, the rope digging into my skin. I can feel someone watching me and I shift my eyes to the corner of the room where a small chair sits. Robbie has been seated there the entire time, watching me. It's sickening.

"Why are you doing this?" I ask, hysterically.

Robbie leans forward in the chair, his elbows resting on his knees. "I told you, I made a mistake before, but we have a second chance now. I was confused, but we are meant to be together, Bryce. I'm the only one who will ever be able to accept your body the way it is now."

I squeeze my eyes closed, tuning him out. Manipulation, his favorite game. "I have to go to the bathroom," I mutter, upset with myself. I can't hold it any longer.

"No problem! Let me go grab the bucket," Robbie says hopping up.

"Robbie, please, if you really want to give this a solid try, you're going to have to loosen the reigns a little. I promise I won't run." I will say just about anything to end up in the bathroom.

He seems to be pondering his options when he finally gives in, nodding his head. He unties me from the bedposts, freeing my wrists and ankles, and then walks me into the bathroom. "Do you mind?" I ask staring at the open door, but Robbie just smiles back at me.

I know that I can't hold it any longer, and that I'm going to have to suck up my pride and pee in front of him. I keep my eyes trained on the ceiling as I sit on the toilet and do my business. I feel naked. When I am finally finished, Robbie walks me back to the bedroom, where he insists I lay down so I can be tied back up.

"You don't have to do this," I say gently. I know the only way I am going to get a leg up is if I play his game. Even though it makes me physically sick to do so, I run my hand through his longer hair and over his unruly beard. "You have no idea how much I have missed you," I lie.

He cocks his head to the side. "You have?"

I nod. "I've been so depressed and lost without you. I lie in my bed and cry myself to sleep every single day." I pause, exhaling sharply. "Why did you leave me?"

He runs his fingers across my face gently, tingles prickling up my back. "I thought you hated me. You're not mad?"

I shake my head. "No. How could I be? We're soulmates, remember?"

His shoulders relax and he leans in to kiss me. I can think of no better torture, but if I want to live, I have to play along. I give him all the passion he would expect and even suck on his bottom lip a little for good measure.

My eyes travel down his body to his right hand where he is clutching his gun tightly. I grip his shirt between my fingers and pull him down toward me. "Put the gun down," I whisper seductively into his ear. "I want you," I add in knowing it will put a fire under his ass.

He sets the gun down and then climbs on top of me on the bed. The position of our bodies still feels familiar, but now I feel terrified as well. Robbie rips off his shirt and throws it on the ground. His eyes are dark and cold. "Make love to me, Robbie. We don't have sex, remember? We make love."

The idea of being intimate with Robbie makes me sick to my stomach, but the dangerous look in his eyes tells me that it isn't going to be gentle. He lowers his lips to my neck and as he stays occupied, I reach around his back to the nightstand. He perches himself up on his palms when I slide from beneath him, headed straight for the gun. My fingers curl around it and I hold it up, directly in his face.

Robbie looks shocked. "You don't want to do this."

I cock my head to the side, "I don't? See...that's where you're wrong. You made me weak when you tried to take my life from me, but I'm taking it back now." I stand tall, stepping off of the bed.

Robbie lifts himself up as well, taking a hesitant step toward me with his hand outstretched, reaching for the gun. He's going to have to pry it from my cold, dead fingers. When he gets too close for comfort, I don't think about the consequences, just pull the trigger, a bullet dislodging from the gun and hitting Robbie right in the chest. He staggers backward, falling onto his back on the floor.

"You shot me!" he exclaims surprised.

I drop the gun to the ground with a thud. I'm as shocked as he is. I've never hurt another human being in my life, at least not on purpose. He is breathing heavily, his eyes rolling backward. I know he will die unless I call the police. I step back toward the bed and take a seat on top of the gold comforter. Robbie looks so harmless as he bleeds out onto the ground. He's not intimidating, and for the first time in a long time, a weight feels like it's being lifted off of my shoulders. As soon as Robbie takes his final breath, I go searching through the house for a phone to call 911, still shaking uncontrollably.

Fifteen: Progress Report

"I know we've already been through this, but I have to ask you again, what took place in your old house?" Officer Jenkins scoots in her chair, readying herself with a notepad and pen.

I'm tired of explaining it. I feel like I am having to relive the nightmare over and over again. I know I have a right to an attorney, but the only thing I can think of right now is how badly I want to see my mother and father. I know the police called them, but the waiting is torture.

I glance up at the two way mirror facing me in the interrogation room. I know someone is outside listening in; probably watching me and my behaviors. *Maybe I should be punished for this.* When has killing someone ever been okay?

"Bryce?" Officer Jenkins pulls me out of my trance.

I rub my hand over my face, sighing. "Can I have some coffee?" I ask.

Officer Jenkins exhales deeply, standing up. "Sure, I'll be right back."

She heads for the door, her long strawberry

blond ponytail bouncing back and forth.

"Bryce?" I hear my mother's familiar voice outside the door. I jump up and run toward the sound. She is standing beside my father and Mikey, and they all have matching worried expressions. I rush to my mother first, feeling comfort and safety the moment her arms wrap around me. I am shaking from happiness and fear and she squeezes me tighter, rubbing her hand soothingly up and down my back.

"Are you okay?" she asks, glancing down at me.

I keep my arms tightly wrapped around her as I burrow my head further under her chin. "I will be."

I release her from the tight embrace and my father wraps his arms around me, pulling me into him. "Your mother and I were so worried when you didn't come home. I'm sorry I couldn't protect you," he says softly pressing his lips to the top of my hair. I pull away, tears trailing down my face. "It's okay, Daddy, I learned how to protect myself."

Mikey surprises me by wrapping his small arms around me. I can't remember the last time he hugged me. It feels strange, but it feels nice.

We remain at the police station for another hour while my parents are witness to the story. After the police have retained all the answers needed, they allow me to leave with my family. I have blood on my clothes and the minute I get inside our house, I race upstairs and into my bathroom, stripping myself of the violent reminder. I climb into the shower, letting the scalding hot water trail down my spine. *I can't believe it's finally over.* No more having to look over my shoulder. No more fearing for my safety.

I have no idea what the outcome is going to be for the police department and if I will eventually be arrested for killing Robbie, but they have all the documentation from the hell he put me through. They took photos of my bruised wrists and ankles, and I am pleading self-defense. Officer Jenkins showed me kindness for the entire ordeal I'd been through. Something tells me that she has a very interesting history.

The only thing I really know at this moment is I no longer have someone trying to kill me; someone obsessed with taking away my freedom. I don't have to be the victim any longer. I plan to take advantage of that. After my skin is prune-like from sitting in the shower for so long, I exit my bathroom in my bathrobe and head for my bedroom. Once I have dressed, I open my door and my mother is ascending the stairs. "Hey honey," she says with a small smile. "Tyson called while you were in the shower."

"He did?" I ask. I had nearly forgotten about everything Robbie did to him as well. She nods. I debate calling him back, but think better of it. My life is mine again. I need to start acting like it. I throw on my warm wool peacoat and rush past my mother and down the stairs.

"Bryce?" she calls out from behind me.

I stop in place, spinning around.

"I'm really sorry we weren't there for you," she says, her eyes filling with tears.

"Oh, Mom!" I race to her, throwing my arms around her small figure. "Please don't blame yourself. It's finally over, and that's all I could really ask for."

She cries into my hair for a few seconds before pushing me toward the door. "Go. Tyson is worried about you."

I heed her advice and head straight for my car which my parents brought back for me last night. I'm thankful I didn't have to return to the scene of the crime right away. I could use some distance for a bit.

When I make it to the hospital, Tyson is shifted away from the door, watching television. His chest is rising and falling with his peaceful breaths and I take a moment to just admire him. I don't know why I was so stubborn before. Even though he's a bit younger than me, I feel like he's made for me. He's handsome, charismatic, charming, and tough. I wouldn't have had the chance to get to know him if it weren't for everything Robbie did to make my life a living hell. So while I wish we had met under different circumstances, I know that he entered my life for a reason. I guess we can call it fate. He was brought into my life to remind me that I didn't have to be a slave to my fear, and I believe I was brought into his to show him what true love could really feel like.

He shifts his eyes lazily to me when I accidentally knock a paper to the ground and hurriedly pick it up, putting it back in its rightful place. Tyson's eyes widen the moment he realizes it's me. "Are you okay?" he asks, concerned.

I don't bother responding, instead just run to him and carefully embrace him. I just want to savor the moment. "So, funny thing about your iPod and clothes…" I trail off, choking on a sob.

He pulls me in tighter, comforting me in his warm embrace. I'm still a mess from everything that went down in the last couple of days.

"Is it over?" he asks as he releases me.

I nod as he swipes a tear from under my eye. He pulls me into him, pressing his lips gently against mine. I can feel warm tears trailing down his face which are landing on our lips. I've never felt closer to him in my entire life.

* * *

One Month Later – December

"You look happy," Linda says, pointing at my wide grin.

"I am happy," I reply, sucking in a deep breath. "I'm not a victim anymore. I got my life back."

"You got the boy," Linda adds.

"That too." I smile even brighter. I never thought in a million years my life could be this incredible. I never thought I could ever feel this way again.

"Bryce, I am so impressed and overjoyed by the progress you've made in such a short amount of time. I am really going to miss you, but I finally feel like you are ready to move forward with your life." Tears are forming at the back of her eyes and I jump up and race to embrace her.

"Thank you so much for everything. If it weren't for you, I'd still be hiding out in my room." I hug her tightly, meaning every word.

She rubs her hand up and down my back similar to the way my mom does. It's comforting and familiar. "Alright, goodbye Bryce," Linda says with a solemn expression as she packs up her notepad and pen for which will be her last time.

I follow her out to the front door where my mother and father are waiting. My mother and father share a mix of expressions: fear, happiness, and confliction. My mother wraps her arms around Linda without giving her time to prepare. Her arms are pinned to her side awkwardly. "Thank you so much for everything."

My father stands beside her tall and proud. He looks over at me winking. "Thank you, Linda," he says as my mother releases her. She nods and then glances back at me. "It's your turn now. Don't forget to live."

I breathe in her words, closing my eyes. When I open them again, she's gone. I'm really going to miss Linda. She's one of the only people who know what really happened to me. She is one of the only people I've talked to about everything.

I know I am going to be okay. I'm going to be better.

Sixteen: Experiencing Life for What it's Worth

"I wasn't sure what I was going to say to you when I finally found the courage to come here. I wasn't sure I'd ever find the courage, but life is about overcoming obstacles and facing our fears. So, I'm here…if you had it your way, I'd be ten feet under." I pause, taking a deep breath.

"You know, I should hate you. I should blame you for all the things you put me through. But honestly I pity you. The thing is, if it wasn't for everything you did to me, I don't know that I would have even found the strength inside myself, so thank you. If it wasn't for you, I wouldn't have met Tyson. I finally understand what it's like to be treated like a human being. I didn't understand at the time that pulling someone's hair until it bleeds and spitting in their face was not normal. You called me a worthless piece of shit so many times, I was beginning to believe it. And then he came around. At first, it was just simple drop in's. Maybe a quick hi or hello in the driveway, and then it became borrowing eggs and flour." I breathe in deeply, looking around as the wind whips my hair all over the place.

"I was so thankful for a distraction. Any distraction that could help me forget my everyday life. Tyson was such a sweetheart and when I was with him, the world around us dissipated. I knew the feelings I had were wrong, but I was so unhappy. The idea of seeing his smile at any point through my day gave me the adrenaline I needed not to lie in bed and never wake up. He always seemed so happy to see me, it gave me butterflies." I pick at the grass next to his headstone.

"You lit me on fire for trying to leave you. You took everything away from me in that moment, and you won. You damaged me beyond repair for a very long time. I still have trouble looking in the mirror. My insecurities are sky high. I don't know how anyone could find me attractive now. I've lived in fear for far too long. But you know what, I forgive you, because if I don't, I won't be able to forget you." I lay a single black rose onto his headstone. It reads: Robbie Jared Wagner, 4/4/1988 – 11/13/2015, son and brother.

There was a service held by his family last week. I'm not sure how many people attended, but I'm happy his family had an avenue to say goodbye to him. No matter what he put me through, no one deserves to die. I wholeheartedly believe that.

For too long, I've been paralyzed in fear that if I even entertained the idea of being with Tyson again, Robbie would somehow find me and finish the job. But I realize now that everything happens for a reason. Tyson is my reason for breathing, my everything. The timing has never been right until now. I'm in love with my best friend and it's incredible; better than I ever could have imagined.

* * *

Two Months Later - February

"You got that?" Tyson motions with his head toward the box I am carrying.

I shift the weight of the box between both my arms and nod my head. "There's a little more in the U-Haul."

Tyson nods in understanding and makes his way over to the U-Haul in the driveway. I stop for a moment, admiring the house we will be living in. It is an off-white color with bright blue trim. It is only one story, but a little over 1000 square feet. There are two bedrooms and two bathrooms. It was built in the 1930's.

If you would have asked me a month ago what my future held, I'm not sure I could have predicted this. I was finally ready to fly the coop from my parents' house, and Tyson was ready for a change, so we decided to take a leap of faith and move in together. We're inseparable enough as it is, so making it official is the next step.

I have returned back to school, and I am halfway to my associate's degree. I've decided I want to be a counselor, so it'll be quite a bit more school before I'm finished. Tyson is still attending ASU, and is excited to share the campus with me.

The box begins weighing me down and I scurry up the walkway and through the front door. I drop it almost immediately after coming through the door and slowly begin making my way to the room which will be our bedroom. Exhausted, I fall onto the white carpet and close my eyes.

Not even five minutes later I hear footsteps and then Tyson's deep voice saying, "hey, no fair!" He falls down beside me and I instantly pull him into me. He is wearing my favorite cologne of his, the one that makes me do crazy things. He presses his lips to mine and I live within every moment. I don't ever want to forget the way I feel today.

He rubs his hand over my clothes, careful not

to cross any boundaries I have. We've been enjoying one another's company for quite a while now, but Tyson has been an absolute saint. He hasn't pressured me to do anything I'm not comfortable doing. I knew there would eventually come a time when I was going to have to come to terms with the fact that Tyson was going to see my body, but I figured the longer I kept him occupied with our make-out sessions, the less time he would have to witness it firsthand.

Things have been heating up each and every time we are alone. I think I'm ready to show him my scars. I jump up extending my hand out for Tyson. He grabs it and stands as well. I lead him to the bathroom which is attached to our room, and turn on the shower.

His eyes look surprised, yet playful, intrigued, yet timid. We've never gone this far before. He's wondering if I'm ready.

"Tyson, I love you, and it's because I love you that I want to show you something." He nods, his eyes trained on me.

"You've seen a little bit of it already when I've worn short sleeve shirts or maybe a skirt, but I want you to know what you are getting into," I warn him.

His eyes look sad as I slowly pull off my t-shirt and close my eyes, scared to see his reaction. It's so quiet a pin could drop, but I can hear his heavy breathing. He hasn't said a word, but I feel his fingers grace my skin, tracing the burns. My eyes flutter open, and he is still staring at my damaged skin with a solemn face. "God, you're beautiful," he says seriously, pulling me into him. My heart is beating wildly. *He's not disgusted by me?*

He reaches for my pants and I stop him by grabbing his hand. "Wait," I say. "It's worse down there..." I trail off, glancing at my legs.

Tyson shrugs kissing me quickly. "I don't care what it looks like, don't you get it? I care about how you make me feel."

I nod, unsure of whether I buy his words or not. This time when he reaches for the button of my pants, I don't stop him. Slowly, he wiggles them off of my body and I once again shield my eyes. I feel fingers wrapping around my hand. "Bryce," Tyson says softly.

I squint open my eyes slowly, terrified that he is being all too calm about this. When we finally lock eyes, he leans in, pressing his palm flat against my chest and pressing me against the glass case of the shower. He lowers his lips to mine in a sensual kiss and it takes all my fears away.

He moves his lips over my scars, one by one kissing them gently, making me feel loved. "You're beautiful," Tyson whispers into my ear. I lean into his hot breath.

He takes his hand to my underwear, rubbing overtop of it, pressing his lips to the base of my neck. The sensual way he is sucking on my skin is sending tingles down my thighs.

Steam is rising from the shower, clouding the mirrors. I reach for Tyson's shirt and rip it off, throwing it to the ground. He follows suit, discarding his pants. We are both now in our underwear. Tyson presses me up against the glass, grinding himself against me and I shudder from the excitement. He runs his hands over my bra and then reaches in, pulling out my medium-sized breasts. He twirls my nipple between his thumb and pointer finger, sending electrical impulses down my thighs.

He unhooks my black bra dropping it with the rest of my clothes and takes one of my breasts in his mouth, pulling the nipple between his teeth and sucking on it. I can feel the wetness pooling between my legs. He reaches for my last piece of clothing and tosses it amongst the rest of our combined clothes. I slip one finger in between his abdomen and his boxer-briefs and pull it away from his body. He kisses me with tongue, showing me he enjoyed my last move.

Tyson climbs into the shower, pulling me in behind him. He maneuvers himself so that I am underneath the showerhead. He presses against me, the water pounding down his back. "I wanted you so badly, but I didn't want to let anyone down. I wasn't a home-wrecker, and couldn't stand drama."

I push him away gently. If I had told Tyson I had feelings for him and he had felt the same way, maybe I wouldn't have been alone with Robbie. Maybe he wouldn't have resorted to such violence. Then again, the same man kidnapped and tortured me, so I am probably wrong.

"We're here now," I say softly. "Don't blink and miss your chance." I can feel the firmness of his manhood against my inner thighs. The temperature rising for more reasons than just the steam.

He slips one finger inside of me, and I grip my fingernails into his shoulder, letting him know that I enjoy the abruptness. Not long after, he slips a second finger in and my body subconsciously begins working out my leg muscles as I bob up and down on them, building the friction. His thumb begins massaging my clit and I'm positive I'm going to come. I push him away from me roughly, wanting to wait until we can climax together. Sex feels more intimate that way.

I wrap my fingers around his dick and move my hand expertly up and down the shaft, my thumb rubbing the very tip of it every time. Tyson's head falls back slowly, as he enjoys the feeling of my hands taking care of him. I squeeze and pull his balls, maneuvering them in circles in the palm of my hand.

His breathing is heavy and constant, and I know he's fighting a battle of his own. He grabs my hips and spins me around so that I'm facing away from him. He grabs my hands and positions them on the wall of the shower. He's moving my body like I'm a puppet, but I'm enjoying every moment of it. He reaches below my hips and pulls my butt towards him, then he presses down on my lower back, angling my body at a position allowing him entry.

I close my eyes, taking a deep breath, knowing that I haven't been with anyone since Robbie. This is intimate, this is real. *I'm going to have sex with my best friend.* My heart goes into overdrive as I worry if I will perform well…if he will like it.

His dick pushes through from behind and into me. The friction of my natural body liquids, how tight I am, and how thick he is feels like heaven. I'm on the pill, so I love not having that barrier between our bodies. He starts slow and gentle, feeling me out, finding his rhythm.

It feels like he is ripping me apart in the most beautiful way. He gains momentum as I react to how good he feels inside of me. I can feel the tidal wave coming. It's traveling up my body, rising from the depths. He feels amazing. It won't be long.

My moans grow louder as he thrusts faster and deeper. I'm digging my fingers into the walls, trying to hold on. I can feel his body tensing up from behind me. We're in sync. He comes inside of me, but still thrusts a few more times until my body shudders beneath his. I collapse onto the seat of the shower, breathing deeply.

He leans against the opposite wall, his arms across his chest. He is smiling.

I look up at him curiously. "What?"

He laughs, shaking his head. "Nothing."

"No, seriously, what?" I push.

He stares back at me. "I knew it was going to

be good…I just didn't know it was going to be *that* good.

I smile victoriously. "Good to know I haven't lost my skills."

He shakes his head. "No way. You're…you're incredible, Bryce." He takes a few steps toward me, and then crouches down so we are at the same level. He reaches his hand out, pushing my wet hair behind my ears.

"I love you," I blurt out, unable to hold it back any longer.

Tyson's eyes grow wide and then teary. "What did you say?"

I reach my hands up, circling them around his neck. "I said that I love you, Tyson."

He reaches out, caressing my face. His lips meet mine almost immediately with a sense of urgency and hunger. "I fucking love you, Bryce," he says as he pulls away. "I'm sorry for being a jerk."

I shake my head back and forth. "I'm sorry that I wasn't ready. I'm sorry I wasn't honest with you."

He reaches under my legs, keeping them

spread, but pulling me closer to him.

"What are you doing?" I ask, smiling.

"Well, I'm giving you the apology you deserve," he replies in a cocky tone and then I feel his warm breath on my inner thigh.

Oh, dear.

*   *   *

"On a scale of one to ten, how nervous are you?" Tyson asks, running his hand gently through my hair.

We are cuddled up on the bed together, mentally preparing for my court appearance today.

I breathe in deeply. "Eleven."

"What's the worst that could happen?" Tyson props himself up on his elbow, staring at me questioningly.

"I could spend the rest of my life in jail for killing that son of a bitch," I choke on a sob.

Tyson pulls me in closer, comforting me. "He tried to kill you, Bryce, twice, you were acting in self-defense. Just be you today. Show them how what he put you through affected your life."

I nod, nuzzling my face into his chest.

"Think of it this way, if you do go to jail, I'll have a prison wife," Tyson jokes, raising his eyebrows.

I smack him in the chest. "Oh, you shut up!"

Today is the first day of the rest of my life. I'm either going to spend the rest of my life being punished for a crime I committed, or I am going to be given a second lease on life. I'm terrified how the jury will swing.

"Seriously, though," Tyson's voice grows serious. "I'm with you every step of the way. You ready to get going?"

I sigh, my eyes darting around our bedroom. I love this new home we've created. I may never see it again, so I savor the time I have left. "Yeah, it's time."

He took away your life – you fought to get it back. There's honor in that. I hope the jury will *hear* my story.

*   *   *

"Ms. Turner, I've never seen quite an impact as I have today during your trial. Your story was, unbelievable. You had jury members in tears within the first ten minutes. I can't even begin to imagine the hell you have been living in. The hell Mr. Baxter put you through. You're a very beautiful and courageous girl, Ms. Turner, I think life dealt you a rough hand, and I think you've been dealing with it as best as you can. I think you were a good girl who met the wrong guy. Mr. Baxter deserved the highest level of punishment, and I wholeheartedly believe he got it. Karma is a peculiar thing. As for the charges of Involuntary Manslaughter, we the jury find you innocent on all counts. Furthermore, we are willing to open a countersuit against the state of Arizona for failing to locate and detain Mr. Baxter before he caused any further physical damage to you and your loved ones."

The courtroom erupts with cheers and it startles me. Tyson jumps up from the bench behind me, wrapping his arms around me, joining in on the victory celebration.

As we exit the courthouse, there are news stations and reporters scattered about, all yelling different questions at me. Flashes are going off every few seconds as my picture is being taken over and over again.

"Bryce! Bryce!" One voice sticks out among the rest. "What are you going to do now that you are free?"

I step up to the microphone the reporter is holding out toward me. "I'm going to live my life."

Other reporters are shouting out their questions, but we maneuver past them and back into Tyson's Bug.

Tyson glances at me before hitting the gas. "You were amazing."

I blush. "Thanks. I couldn't have done it without you."

"Where to now?" he asks, his eyes darting between me and the road ahead.

"I don't care. Surprise me."

Tyson grins back at me and then takes off with a jolt.

I have the rest of my life ahead of me. No more tip-toeing through life. It's my turn to experience it.

Our love was epic. Our pain was inevitable.
We shared demons, but his were always darker than mine.
We always fought them head on.
Until tragedy changed him, and he lost his way.
I'll do anything to help him find his way back home.
Things won't be the same until he's just Caspian again.

Ginger and Caspian's relationship has always had its ups and downs. Now their greatest loss might bring them their greatest gift. As they work out their grief, accept their loss, and figure out how to move forward, they'll discover if their love can stand the test of time.

This is a standalone novella and a spin-off series from the Hollywood Timelines series featuring Caspian Norwood and Ginger Teague, characters introduced in The One Thing

just CASPIAN

Briana Gaitan

All rights reserved. No part of this book may be reproduced or transmitted in any form or by any means, electronic or mechanical, including photocopying, recording or by any information storage and retrieval system, without written permission from the author, except for the inclusion of brief quotations in a review.

www.brianagaitan.info

www.facebook.com/booksbybree

Copyright © 2015 by Briana Gaitan

Lyrics from "Ginger" used with permission by Josh O'brien.

First Edition, 2015

This is a work of fiction.

All characters appearing in this book are fictitious. Any resemblance to real persons living or dead are purely coincidental. This book identifies product names and services known to be trademarks, registered trademarks, or service marks of their respective holders. They are used throughout this book in an editorial fashion only.

For My mom, for teaching how to love reading.

Thank you for picking up Just Caspian!

Sign up for my mailing list wwwbrianagaitan.info for giveaways, exclusive content, and new book news.

Other books by Briana Gaitan

The Last Thing

The One Thing

Bash

Maria

Ethereal Underground Trilogy

THE ARRIVAL

"I'm not a rock star. I'm just a guy. Just Caspian." -Caspian

I put the car in park and roll down the window so I can get a better look at the dirt road looming ahead of us.

"All the way down there?" I ask, quite certain we're lost. The lonesome road looks to stretch on for miles, fading into the horizon as the sun peeks over the Rocky Mountains. New Mexico is pleasantly warm, but the terrain is brown and boring. I make a few more mental comparisons to LA before rolling the window back up. This trip is long overdue, and it should be under better circumstances, but it's not.

Caspian sits up from his reclined seat, rubs his red eyes, and looks around.

"Yeah, it's a few miles down." His voice is rough as if he's been screaming all night.

"Keep going. It's the only house for miles. Can't miss it."

I tap my nails along the steering wheel for a moment before pulling onto the road. It's the type of road that people use to hide dead bodies or grow pot. The type that leads to nowhere except someone's extreme privacy. Is this what people mean when they say 'living off the grid?' How do they get delivery all the way out here? What if they get a pizza craving in the middle of the night?

We've been driving in silence for hours, and Caspian is teetering on the edge of something dark. I can tell from the way his knee bounces up and down and how he keeps rubbing his hand on his jeans. He's a bundle of nerves, but not the excited kind. Every once in a while, he'll run his hands down his face and let out a horrible groan, as if he were trying to wake up from a nightmare. Sad thing is, this is the worst kind of nightmare. The cold sweat kind that keeps your heart beating for hours after it's over. I try to empathize with what he's feeling, but I've never had to go through something like this before. I'm too afraid I'll say the wrong thing, but mostly afraid of saying nothing. I don't want to be the kind of girlfriend that can't make him feel better. Best thing I can do is put on my par acting skills and be here for him.

He perks up as a large adobe style home appears in the distance. His nervous twitches get even worse and for a moment I'm afraid the car will topple over from all his fidgeting. I'm glad we're here though. I ran out of coffee a few hours ago, and I'm not used to pulling all-nighters. A girl needs her beauty sleep, know what I mean?

As the car stops, I reach out to push his blond hair off his forehead. He rewards me with his signature goofy grin, the only grin I've seen from him since the call came. The call that made us drop everything and make the twelve-hour drive from our house in LA to his parents' place just outside of Albuquerque. When he realizes what he's doing, the smile fades, and with the loss of that momentary smile, my heart sinks further into my chest.

"Thank you, Deena. Thank you for coming with me."

He's the only one who calls me by my given name. To the rest of the world, I am Ginger. Ginger Teague, soap opera actress and most recently, movie star. He kisses the back of my hand before taking a deep breath and opening the car door. I do the same, trying to stay calm. Now that I've had a moment to appreciate New Mexico, it's actually kind of breathtaking. Picturesque in a way. Fresh air and a clear sky. There's only one downside, the place is kind of dusty, but the house is so distracting I hardly notice the lack of greenery. It's huge. I mean, huge in a way that you'd expect a billionaire to live here. One would never expect this to be the home of a dentist and a simple schoolteacher. *Business must be good.*

It could be a southwestern castle with its vista architecture and large stone walls, but it has a modest homey feel to it, just like Caspian's whole family.

We reach the entrance, and like a man on a mission, Caspian throws the front doors open. Without missing a beat, he falls into his father's waiting arms as his mother looks on. The scene is heartbreaking and humbling. All I can do is stand back and let them have their moment.

"Pops," he mumbles into the older man's shoulder. This should be a touching moment. Father and son reunited after so long, but the somberness of it all only cause tears to form in the corner of my eyes.

The impromptu family reunion continues as Caspian's other brothers enter to greet him. First Peter then Ed take their turn embracing him. All the brothers are named after Pearl's favorite books *The Chronicles of Narnia*. Finally his mother, Pearl, looking exhausted, wipes her hands on her apron and gathers him into her arms. I shift uncomfortably regretting all the coffee I'd consumed on the road. What should be a beautiful reunion is marred by the absence of Tirian, the oldest Norwood brother that I'll never get to meet.

Pearl holds her hand out and motions for me to join in on the family group hug. I give her a tight smile and move closer. My family was never the touchy feely kind, so their embracing takes some getting used to. I've only met them a few times, but they've never excluded me. Right now, I want to be excluded. It feels wrong to share in their mourning. I know that sounds selfish, and maybe I am, but I didn't know Tirian. I wish I had, he sounded like a wonderful man. Nonetheless, in our few short months together, I never got the pleasure. Tirian always missed family holidays and vacations because of work obligations.

"Take care of my baby boy. Take care of him," she whispers into my ear. "He's going to take this harder than the rest."

She's right. Caspian is the most sensitive out of all his brothers. Edmund is the hopeless romantic and a dentist like his father while Peter is the fatherly one. To me, anyway. Caspian? Caspian feels too much or too little. There is no in between for him. This will be one of the cases where he'll feel too much and be overwhelmed by the velocity of it all. I excuse myself to the bathroom so they can have their family time. You know, discuss personal matters and cry.

When I'm finished relieving myself, I find everyone gathered in the kitchen around a large round oak table.

"How did it happen?" Caspian asks as I sit down next to him.

"This all feels so unreal. He just got back from another trip," James' voice cracks, and he pauses for a moment to remove his wire spectacles and wipe the tears from his eyes, the same crystal blue orbs that all the Norwood brothers share. I only knew the facts about Tirian. He was a pro bono doctor. Highly respected. He and his family moved from place to place to provide health care to those in need. They'd lived all over the world. From the far reaches of Africa to an orphanage in Mexico.

"He and Alyne went shopping for Ryker's birthday. Some guy at the mall began shooting. We don't know all the details, and we don't know why. Dozens were injured. Tirian was shot —" James trails off, and Pearl begins stacking waffles on everyone's plates. My eyes wander over to the marble countertops that are filled with pastries, cakes, and croissants. It's clear that Pearls been busying herself in the kitchen to take her mind off the loss of her son.

James inhales deeply before speaking again. "He died instantly. Alyne is in the hospital. Gunshot to the chest. We're not sure if she's—if she's gonna make it."

"Why are we here and not at the hospital?" Caspian tries to get up, but his father puts a hand on his shoulder, sitting him back down.

Pearl sniffles into her apron. "Well, apparently in-laws aren't considered family so we can't be in her room. We were in the waiting room most of the night, but someone has to take care of Bella. I don't think she quite understands what's going on. "

Caspian nods as he struggles to calm down. "Where is my little Bella-bee anyway? I want to see her."

"Still asleep."

"And the man who shot Tirian?"

"Dead. The police gunned him down."

Caspian's face changes expressions a few times. It's hard to read him, but I think he was hoping that the gunman being dead would ease his pain, but it doesn't seem to be working.

With somber faces, everyone moves to hold hands. The reason why goes over my head, and for a moment I think we're all going to sing a song. Caspian is a musician, after all.

Maybe this is where his love of music came from.

"We're saying grace," Caspian whispers as he takes my hand in his.

I've never said grace before, especially not holding anyone's hand. Even though I grew up in the Bible belt, my family wasn't very religious. We were more of the holiday Catholics. Christmas, Easter, confirmations, baby christenings. You know, the events where my father thought alcohol might be served. Caspian had warned me his father was pretty into the God thing, which is surprising because Caspian isn't spiritual at all.

I follow their lead and take Peter's hand in my other. I bow my head, same as them.

"Dear Heavenly Father, please give us the strength to get through this terrible day. Help us to remember that everything happens for a reason, and that Tirian is in a better place. Please—" He's silent for several more seconds, and we wait for the rest of his prayer that never comes. Eventually, he mutters amen.

The rest of breakfast goes by in a blur. I'm tired, nervous, and eager to get some sleep. I've spent the past week working on different gigs. Promotions and special appearances while Caspian stays at home, producing and writing songs for different friends. Though Caspian and I have been together for five months, being around his family is new to me.

After we eat, Pearl won't let us help clean up. Instead, she insists we get some rest. Caspian leads me down a long hall towards my room. Caspian will be staying in his old room next door.

"Don't they know we live together?" I hiss when I realize the sleeping arrangement.

"My parents are a bit old fashioned."

He sets our bags on the ground and pulls a few blankets from the antique wardrobe in the corner.

"Hello? It's like a million degrees outside. I don't want a blanket. Why are you ignoring me? Talk to me." I grab onto his shirt as he walks past me preparing the room. He pushes me off and straightens out the collar.

"Not now, Ginger. I need to get some sleep. I'll be in the next room."

I make one last attempt to get him to look at me. "Why are you shutting me out? Let me help you. Please?"

He pauses, head down, shoulders slumped. Before I know what's happening, he's in my arms. I squeeze him as the sobs flow from his body. I have to keep from letting my own fall.

"My big brother," he cries. Normally, I'd wince at the fact that his tears are staining a four-hundred dollar blouse, but not today. Today I'd gladly donate any piece of my wardrobe to catch his tears and ease his pain. He's the man who saved me. He always saw the good in me. He saved me from heading down a bad path. When my life revolved around parties and being selfish and reckless, he showed me there was more to life.

I want to be here for him, but I'm not good at this type of stuff. Disappointed in myself, I bite my bottom lip and try to think of the best way to comfort him. What can I say? The words don't come easily, so eventually I settle on the easy way out.

"I'm so sorry, Cas. I'm not sure what to say."

He takes a deep breath and pulls himself together. "Nothing. You need to sleep. You've been driving all night."

My eyelids are heavy, but I still have a few remaining spurts of caffeine running through my veins that would prevent me from falling asleep right away. I gave up so much this weekend to be here for him, but now that the time has come, I don't feel like he's leaning on me. I don't feel like I'm the best person for him to lean on. People bond over life experiences. He and I bonded over our struggles with the bottle. No one I've ever cared for has died. I just don't know what to do to help.

"Cas? Are you okay?"

He looks at me like I've just asked the stupidest question in the world. "Okay? Okay is a term used to describe something average. An okay day or an okay movie. I might say, 'she looks okay' or 'the food is okay.' I could never describe the way I feel as okay. I am not okay. I'm not sure I'll ever be okay."

"Okay, I mean, all right."

He squeezes my hand before leaving the room.

I grab my pajamas and head to the bathroom to wash up. When I'm finished, I climb into the huge bed and lay down. The room is decorated plainly, but everything is still exquisite. From the carved crosses on the wooden doors to the stained glass window, I'm afraid to touch anything. That's okay, I don't need to touch anything, I need to sleep and after tossing and turning for a long time, I'm there.

Acknowledgements

This is for any girl, woman, man, or child that has been through this. Who can relate to the abuse because they lived through it. I dedicate this story to you. No one ever deserves to be treated like they are nothing.

You hold the strength inside yourself. Don't settle.

Don't forget—if you're not doing something you love, you're not really living.

Kira Adams

About the author:

Krista Pakseresht has always been a dreamer. From the first time she opened her eyes. Creating worlds through words is one thing she is truly talented at. She specializes in Young adult/New adult romance, horror, action, fantasy, and non-fiction under the pen name Kira Adams. She is the author of the Infinite Love series, the Foundation series, the Darkness Falls series, and the Looking Glass series.

Books by Kira Adams:

The Infinite Love Series
Learning to Live (Ciera & Topher)
My Forever (Madalynne & Parker)
Beautifully Broken (Jacqueline & Lee)
Against All Odds (Austyn & Avery)

The Foundation Series
Pieces of Me
The Fighter

Darkness Falls Series
Into the Darkness
Emerging from Darkness

Standalones
A Date with the Devil

Made in the USA
Charleston, SC
29 June 2015